A Candlelight Ecstasy Romance™

"ARE YOU GOING TO OFFER," HE TAUNTED. "OR MUST I PLAY KISS THIEF?"

"Ben, I . . ."

"Okay," he sighed deeply. "Have it your way. But if I have to steal it, I may as well make it worth the effort."

His lips touched hers and the effort he put forth was shattering. Never in her life had Vichy been kissed quite like Ben was kissing her now. There was no slow build-up to possession. His mouth attacked, devoured, vanquished. His arms crushed her softness into submission to the rock hardness of his body. . . .

GAMBLER'S LOVE

Amii Lorin

A CANDLELIGHT ECSTASY ROMANCE™

Published by
Dell Publishing Co., Inc.
1 Dag Hammarskjold Plaza
New York, New York 10017

Dell ® TM 681510, Dell Publishing Co., Inc.
Candlelight Ecstasy Romance™ is a trademark of
Dell Publishing Co., Inc., New York, New York.

ISBN: 0–440–13029–8

Printed in the United States of America
First printing—December 1982

To Our Readers:

We have been delighted with your enthusiastic response to Candlelight Ecstasy Romances™ and we thank you for the interest you have shown in this exciting series.

In the upcoming months, we will continue to present the distinctive, sensuous love stories you have come to expect only from Ecstasy. We look forward to bringing you many more books from your favorite authors and also the very finest work from new authors of contemporary romantic fiction.

As always, we are striving to present the unique, absorbing love stories that you enjoy most—books that are more than ordinary romance.

Your suggestions and comments are always welcome. Please write to us at the address below.

Sincerely,

The Editors
Candlelight Romances
1 Dag Hammarskjold Plaza
New York, N.Y. 10017

GAMBLER'S LOVE

CHAPTER ONE

The drive seemed endless, and by the time she was finally east of the Mississippi, Vichy was beginning to feel like a prisoner of her own car.

A wry smile tugged at her lipstick-free mouth as she consciously loosened her death grip on the abused steering wheel. Being confined inside a Pinto, she decided, was certainly not the ideal way to spend the better part of any week. But it would not be too much longer, and then she would be on the East Coast and damned if she'd ever leave it again.

The highway unfurled before her like a cement ribbon, and Vichy kept her gaze on the sparse mid-week traffic while her mind's eye looked back over the preceding weeks.

She had had it. On what day had she reached that decision? Had it been Tuesday? Wednesday? She couldn't remember, but, then, it really didn't matter. Having reached the decision, Vichy had hung on to it as firmly as she now hung on to the wheel of her car. She had had just about all the traveling she could take, all the smoke-filled rooms, all the night work. Had it really seemed exciting at one time? Yes, she conceded, it really had. A million years ago, when her eyes were still bright with ambition and her dreams were fresh off the assembly line—new. Back before the miles and the years had begun to pile up on her, weighing her down.

The highway blurred and Vichy blinked rapidly to expel the sudden hot moisture that filled her eyes. What good were tears, for heaven's sake? she chided herself scathingly. She was twenty-nine, going on one hundred and two, and if she had learned nothing else, she had learned that tears neither mean nor help anything. Uncurling the fingers of her left hand, she brought them up to her face to brush impatiently at her wet cheeks. *Coffee time,* Vichy told the swimming blue eyes that were momentarily reflected in the rearview mirror by a quick upward glance.

Her eyes scanning the terrain in the distance, Vichy sighed with relief when she spied the familar red-tiled roof of a Howard Johnson restaurant. After parking in the nearly empty macadam lot, she automatically checked her appearance in the mirror, grimacing at her pale reflection before stepping out of the car and locking it. Huddling inside the warmth of her fur-lined suede jacket, she faced the sharp early-November wind and hurried across the lot to the welcoming light streaming through the restaurant's wide plate glass windows.

The restaurant was quiet, as only one table and two counter stools were occupied by customers. Sliding onto a stool near the end of the counter, Vichy ordered coffee from a bored-looking waitress, then lit a cigarette, drawing deeply on the cause of just one of her reasons for her discontent with herself. She had quit smoking over six months ago, only to start up again two weeks previously, when all her unhappiness and restlessness had come to a head. Sighing softly, she smiled wanly at the waitress as the cup of coffee was placed in front of her, then stared moodily into the dark brew.

It was time she went home, she thought tiredly. Long past time. Time to wake up, face reality, no matter how unpalatable. There would be no fame or fortune for her in the entertainment world. Facing that truth had been one of the hardest things she'd ever had to do.

With another soft sigh Vichy lifted her cup. Sipping the hot coffee, she tried to visualize her parents' reaction to her unannounced arrival. Maybe she should have called and told them she was coming home, but, sure of her welcome, she'd plunged into the business of clearing up all the details of her life on the West Coast. She had been determined to leave no loose ends, as she was never going back.

Never going back. The thought stabbed at her mind, the poisoned tip inflicting a searing sense of failure. The known fact that she was only one of thousands who never made the big time brought no relief at all. Dreams die very, very hard.

Moving jerkily with self-impatience, Vichy paid for her coffee and hurried through the darkening afternoon to the now-too-familiar small car. Before sliding behind the wheel, she paused to study the lowering cloud cover. Before too long those enveloping clouds were going to split wide open and drench the landscape. Yet another sigh whispered through her pale lips. The prospect of driving through a downpour was disheartening. Why couldn't the weather have held for a few more days?

Why ask why? Vichy chided herself with a brief flash of humor. Why is a duck? The tiny smile that was just beginning to touch her lips at that nonsensical thought fled with the first cold drop of rain that struck her cheek. Glancing back at the motel complex, Vichy fought a short-lived, go-stay battle with herself. She hated to drive in the rain. The temptation to wait out the weather almost undermined her determination to drive until dusk each day. Squaring her shoulders, she slid behind the wheel and slammed the door closed beside her. Telling herself to get on with it, she turned the key to the ignition.

Two hours later, shoulder muscles tight from gripping the steering wheel, eyes achy from straining to see through the deluge of water pouring out of the sky, Vichy drove off the road with an overwhelming feeling of relief and into the parking lot of a new-looking motel. After checking in, she dropped into the molded plastic chair in the single room and allowed herself the luxury of groaning aloud. She was wet, and she was cold, and still she sat numbly until the sound of the rain slashing against the room's one window drew her attention. By the watch on her wrist it was not yet dusk, but the window she gazed at revealed nothing but darkness beyond its panes. With a shiver, Vichy stood up and walked to the side of the window to pull the cord that drew the flower-patterned drapes together.

Turning her back on the sound of the drops beating on the pane, she removed her sweater, then stepped out of her slacks, shivering again as the sodden material brushed her

12

ankles. Leaving her clothes in a pile next to her wet shoes, she went into the bathroom for a hot shower. After shampooing her rain-bedraggled hair, she stood under the hot spray until she'd stopped shivering completely. Thankfully there were two towels, and before giving herself a brisk rubdown with one, she twined the other around her head turban-style. When she was dry, she considered wrapping the damp towel saronglike around her body, but, then, remembering she'd drawn the drapes, she shrugged and walked nude into the small room. Opening the one valise she'd brought into the motel with her, she removed fresh underwear, a cableknit sweater in a soft pink shade, and a pair of maroon corduroy slacks. As she turned away from the suitcase, Vichy caught her reflection in the wide mirror above the desklike dresser.

Poised like a statue, she studied her reflection impersonally. The five-foot-seven-inch image was not bad, if a little too slender at one hundred and eleven pounds. Although the towel on her head concealed all but a lock of her hair, her matching brows proclaimed the rich dark brown color of her hair. Blue eyes gazed back at her out of an oval-shaped, pale face. Unselfconsciously, Vichy registered the fact that her face was more than just pretty. She was, she admitted, a knockout in the looks department. A twisted smile distorted her soft lips. But all her looks had ever brought her was heartache and advances from the opposite sex, both of which she could easily live without.

One man had even told her she was bewitching. The twist of her lips grew grim and with an impatient shake, she turned away from her mirrored image. Fool that she had been! She'd married that particular man. Even though it had now been almost six years since she'd seen or heard from her former husband, just thinking of him brought a bad taste to her mouth. The memory of that brief, turbulent marriage increased Vichy's feeling of defeat. It seemed she was a loser all the way around.

With a shudder, she forced the feeling away and concentrated on the more immediate need of getting dressed for dinner. She slipped her arms through the straps of the full-cupped, lacy bra and fastened the hooks, then adjusted the garment over her high, well-endowed breasts. After struggling into sheer panty hose, she stepped into her slacks and then into low wedged slingback slip-ons. She removed the towel and pulled the sweater over her head before digging through her suitcase for her blow dryer. Round brush in hand, she dried her hair while brushing the shoulder-length mass into soft waves. A light application of foundation, a quick wisk with the blusher brush, and a faint coating of coral lip gloss, and she was ready to leave the room.

Vichy didn't notice the man's bold stare until she glanced up at the waitress to give her her order. He was sitting with a lovely young woman several tables away from where Vichy sat, yet, even though the woman was speaking to him, his eyes roamed insolently over her body. When his eyes returned to her face, Vichy deliberately glanced away dismissively.

Vichy did not look in his direction again during her stay in the dining room, but his visage remained in her mind. He was so very much like Brad in appearance that without knowing anything about him, she felt sorry for the young woman with him. That man's face was too handsome, almost beautiful, the lower lip too sensuous, the eyes too slumberous. Even though she did not glance in his direc-

14

tion again, Vichy could feel his eyes on her. Irritated with his boorishness and humiliated for his companion, she hurried through her meal, leaving the room without a backward glance.

Back in her room, she draped her damp slacks over the plastic chair, placed her wet shoes near the air vent, and prepared for bed. It was still early, but the tension of driving through the wind-driven rain had left her tired enough, she felt sure, to sleep.

She was wrong. Seeing the man who so resembled Brad had stirred a hornets' nest of memories that crowded in on her attempt to rest.

How excited she'd been about that engagement in Vegas. To be sure, it had been in one of the smaller rooms in one of the smaller hotels, but that hadn't mattered to her. The important thing had been that she was actually there in Las Vegas!

Brad had been in the audience the second night of her engagement. How very impressionable she'd been at twenty-two! And how very gullible. Brad, being ninety percent charm and one hundred percent opportunist, had taken full advantage of her gullibility.

Vichy could still hear the sugar-coated endearments that had rolled so naturally off his lying tongue. Lord! She shuddered in the darkness, thinking that she had actually believed every word he'd uttered. How she must have amused him! And how she paid for her belief and trust.

Within two weeks after that hurried ceremony she had been painfully aware that the only reason Brad had legalized their union was his awareness of the fact that there would be no union without the legality. Very simply, she had been a challenge to him.

Vichy, at twenty-nine, still felt pain for the dreamy-eyed innocent she had been at twenty-two.

"Damn it all!"

Vichy grumbled irritably as she thrust her arm under the pillow and rolled onto her side. She hadn't thought about Brad or their short, disastrous marriage in years! And now, because of an insulting stare from a man who had a striking resemblance to him, she was once again examining one of her failures—the first of many, it seemed.

Sighing defeatedly, Vichy closed her eyes. How did that song go? she wondered, something about never falling in love with a gambling man? She was the living proof of that. She had lavished her first, eager love on that particular gambling man. For almost six months she had existed in a euphoric bubble of bliss. She had trusted him explicitly with her tender, young emotions. Finding him with another woman six months after their marriage had just about destroyed her. It *had* destroyed her trust in men, particularly gamblers.

Now, six years later, the pain she'd felt at that time had long ago subsided. All that remained was a residue of sadness for the trusting young fool she'd been.

A clear case of arrested mentality. A wry smile touched the lips that still possessed a young, vulnerable softness. At twenty-two, and an entertainer in the bargain, she really had been very immature. At the time, she'd been on the supper-club circuit for over a year and, apparently, had learned very little of the cold realities of life. She had been ripe for harvesting by an expert picker. *Comes from being raised in a protected environment,* she now excused the dumb bunny she'd been.

16

The thought of her early environment chased away the bad memories. She was going back to it, soon to stay for good. Not in triumph as she'd vowed she would when she left with such high, warm hopes, but with utter failure dragging at her fashionably high heels. The realization that she'd be welcomed with tears of joy and open arms by her elderly parents and younger sister allowed her to drift into a much-needed sleep. In triumph or defeat, Vichy knew she would be welcomed home joyously. It was her family's way.

Vichy awoke early, and after a quick juice-and-coffee breakfast was back on the road again, thankfully without a glimpse of the cold-eyed young man of the evening before.

Thoughts of the reception awaiting her at her destination kept Vichy's spirits bolstered during the long hours of driving over the following two days. As she crossed the state line into Pennsylvania, she drew a deep breath, telling herself whimsically that she could actually smell a difference in the air of her home state.

Fatigue weighed on her shoulders and her arms felt like lead when, finally, she turned off the macadam road onto the rutted lane that led to her parents' small frame farmhouse, located midway between Lancaster and Ephrata.

Misty-eyed, Vichy gazed at the home of her youth. Sparkling white paint was set off by the dark green trim on the window frames and shutters, a clear indication that her ever-busy father had very recently been at work with a paintbrush.

The yard surrounding the house, her mother's domain, had a pruned, ready-for-winter look, although the chrysanthemums banked against the house still blazed forth in all their rust and gold glory.

Off to the left, its paint every bit as fresh as that on the house, the barn, used now for storage and housing the family's two cars, stood square and solid-looking. Emotion closing her throat, Vichy blinked rapidly as she killed the Pinto's engine and tugged on the hand brake.

Silly, she chided herself, *anyone would think you had been away a dozen years or so when, in fact, it has been less than a year since your last visit.* But, she mentally argued in defense of her tears, brushing at them with trembling fingertips, that was a visit, this is a homecoming.

At the fringes of the lawn to the right of the house, Vichy's searching eyes softened as they came to a halt on the gnarled old apple tree. The sight of a tire, suspended from the tall tree's lowest limb by a sturdy rope, brought a rush of memories clamoring into her mind. A replica of that tire, the first of a long line, had been hung from that branch years before her coming into the world.

That first tire had been affixed for the amusement of the first of the Sweigart brood, Vichy's elder sister, Mattilda— so named for her paternal grandmother.

A tiny smile trembled its way onto Vichy's lips. How Mattie hated her given name! And how she and their brother Josh—named Joshua after their paternal grandfather—had tormented her about it. Yet, her smile deepened; to this day only she and Josh held that exclusive right, except their parents, of course, to the use of her given name.

"Vichy!"

Her younger sister's excited cry scattered the warm

18

memories, and Vichy's eyes shifted to the small figure hurrying across the building's wide front porch.

The runt, as the baby of the four Sweigart offspring had been affectionately dubbed, was the only one of them to inherit their mother's small stature. One inch shy of five feet, she was also the only one of them not named in honor of a demised grandparent, Vichy being named Victoria after her maternal grandmother.

Stepping out of the car, Vichy chuckled softly in remembrance of her baby sister's christening. To her father's wondering shake of his iron gray head, Vichy's mother had named her youngest Bette, after a much-admired movie star!

All remembrance went flying as Bette launched herself into Vichy's arms, chattering thirty to the dozen.

"How did you get here? Well, that's obvious you came in your car, but how come? I mean, it's terrific that you're here, but how come you're here? You look super, but—"

"Whoa, slow down," Vichy cried around a mouthful of laughter. "I'll answer all your questions one at a time, but first, where are the folks?" Keeping a hold on Bette's arms, Vichy leaned back to look questioningly into her sister's heartwrenchingly pretty face.

"Is it Friday?" Bette queried pertly.

"It was when I left the motel this morning," Vichy laughed.

"Well, then, where else would they be?" Bette chided on a return laugh. "They're at the Green Dragon."

"Where else, indeed," Vichy grinned, giving Bette a quick hug. How wonderfully normal and unchanged everything was, even down to Johanna and Luke Sweigart's weekly visit to the large market and auction held on Fridays on the other side of Ephrata.

"They're gonna flip when they get home," Bette broke excitedly into her musing. "Why didn't you let us know you were coming?"

"And miss out on seeing you bounce around like a Mexican jumping bean?" Vichy teased. "How about bouncing your way to the back and helping me unload my stuff?"

Having sold the few pieces of furniture and bric-a-brac she'd accumulated over the last ten years, everything Vichy now possessed was jammed into the hatchback. Never slow on the uptake, Bette ran a sharp-eyed glance over the four suitcases and equal number of small cartons, then lifted her speculative gaze to Vichy.

"You're not going back to California?" she asked on a warmingly hopeful note.

"No," Vichy shook her head. "Except for two short running engagements in Atlantic City over the holidays, I'm home to stay."

The magnitude of Vichy's flat statement was not lost on her twenty-one-year-old sister. Bette knew how badly Vichy had wanted to make a success in the entertainment field, how very hard she'd worked toward her goal.

"You're really quitting?" she asked softly, obviously astonished.

"I'm really quitting," Vichy concurred firmly.

"But—" Bette began in protest.

"We'll talk it out later." Vichy cut in quietly. "But right now I think we'd better unload the car before it gets dark."

Bette talked nonstop while they carried the suitcases and cartons from the car to the bedroom that Vichy had

20

occupied from her fifth year. Up until then she had shared the room with Mattie, who, on reaching her thirteenth year, declared dramatically that she needed privacy. As Josh, then eight, had squatter's rights on the only other bedroom on the second floor, that left the attic. Their father had spent that entire winter measuring, sawing, and hammering in the attic. When, in early March, he was finished, that one large attic had been converted into two small bedrooms and a good-sized storage closet.

On the completion of their father's remodeling, Josh had declared it "neat," and had promptly removed himself and his belongings to the floor above. Josh's bedroom on the second floor had remained empty until Bette made her debut eight years later.

It was fully dark by the time Vichy and Bette had unpacked the valises and lugged them and the cartons up to the storage closet.

"I don't know about you, Vich, but I'm starved," Bette declared as they clattered down the stairs.

"I could do with a cup of coffee," Vichy sighed. "But first I want a hot shower."

"Mom set a container of vegetable soup out to thaw for supper before she left," Bette said, heading for the back-stairs that led directly into the large old-fashioned kitchen. "I'll warm the soup and make a pot of coffee while you have your shower."

"Thanks, hon," Vichy smiled tiredly. "I won't be long."

"Take your time," Bette called from halfway down the stairs. "I wasn't going anywhere."

Sliding her fingers into her long dark brown hair, Vichy walked into her bedroom and came to an abrupt stop on catching her own reflection in the mirror above the dress-

21

er. She was not particularly thrilled with the appearance of the young woman who stared back at her. That woman had a world-weary, defeated look about her.

Her hand stopped in midair, and Vichy's eyes made a minute inspection of her own image. At this moment she looked tired, and every one of her twenty-nine years—plus a few. There were dark smudges in the pale skin under her dulled blue eyes, and her cheeks and lips were totally devoid of color.

Dropping her hand suddenly, she turned away impatiently from that sorry-looking female with a muttered, "That's entertainment?"

The shower went a long way in dispersing the weariness, and a light application of makeup restored at least a semblance of color to her face.

Nose twitching, Vichy followed the mingled aromas of coffee, vegetable soup, and baking powder biscuits to the warm, homey kitchen, somewhat surprised at the sudden sharp edge to her appetite.

Bette was bending over in front of the stove, removing a cakepan of golden-brown biscuits from the oven when Vichy entered the room.

"Showing off your culinary skills?" she teased as Bette straightened and turned to face her. "Or do they come from a box?"

"Bite your tongue," Bette admonished indignantly around a wide grin. "I made these from scratch, as every home economics major should."

"They smell heavenly," Vichy admitted. "So does the soup. Did you create that as well?"

"No," Bette shook her head. "Mom takes the honors for that." After gingerly plucking the hot biscuits out of

22

the cakepan and dropping them into a napkin-lined bread basket, she glanced up, her grin widening. "Mom can still cook circles around me. Except"—she temporized—"where it comes to the *Cordon Bleu* stuff. There I shine." She grinned exaggeratedly. "Not that anyone's impressed with that. As you know, Dad still prefers things like Mother's vegetable soup and pot pies to any of the fancy concoctions I whip up."

Two places were laid on the long, Formica-topped table. A soft smile curved Vichy's lips as she seated herself at her place; for it was *her* place, and had been for as long as she could remember. With her first spoonful of the aromatic soup, she felt she was really, finally home. In Vichy's opinion, no one in the world made vegetable soup quite as good as her mother.

As she savored each successive spoonful, Vichy's gaze roamed lovingly over the large kitchen, which was a combination of up-to-the-minute appliances in old-fashioned country decor.

The line of cabinets above and below the sink were varnished, natural wood, carefully made and fitted by her father's clever hands. Matching wood paneling covered three of the walls. The remaining wall was covered with a bright white-, orange-, and tan-striped wallpaper. The ceiling was open-beamed, the plaster between sparkling white. Everything in the room, as, indeed, the whole house, was showroom clean. The very neatness of the property, both inside and out, was a clear indication that her sixty-year-old mother and sixty-one-year-old father were still fighting fit.

When they'd polished off their soup and most of the

biscuits, Bette filled their cups with steaming, dark coffee and sat a pumpkin pie on the table.

"Fresh baked this morning," Bette announced. "First of the season."

"Looks good enough to eat," Vichy smiled. "I haven't had good pumpkin pie since I was home for Thanksgiving two years ago."

"Well, then, stuff yourself," Bette invited with a proud, sweeping hand motion. "Plenty more where that came from. Mom made four of them this morning."

"Four!" Vichy laughed.

"You know Mom," Bette grinned. "She claims she still can't get used to cooking for only three. She slid one of the pies in the fridge and the other two in the freezer just in case Mattie or Josh drop in with their assorted brood."

"Drop in?" Vichy's eyebrows arched. "Mattie in Williamsport and Josh in Easton, and she expects them to drop in?"

"What can I tell ya?"

Bette's lifted shoulders displayed more elegance than her elocution. "Mom is—well, Mom. She'll never change. She'll probably stop the cortege on the way to her own funeral and declare she can't go just yet, as she has to get supper first."

Although Vichy shook her head in despair at Bette's corollary, she had to smile simply because it was so very near the mark. With cool disregard for the perfection of their mother's handiwork, Bette sliced into the pie.

"Mmmm, heavenly," Vichy murmured around the first bite. "Tastes like home."

"Maybe that's because it is," Bette laughed. "You sound like someone who's been very, very homesick."

24

"Maybe that's because I have been," Vichy admitted seriously. "Homesick, and just plain sick of it all."

Bette was quiet while she removed their empty plates from the table, then, after refilling both coffee cups, she asked softly, "What happened, Vichy?"

"Absolutely nothing," Vichy's smile held a hint of bitterness. "I just, finally, faced the fact that nothing was going to happen." Getting up, she walked to the counter where she'd deposited her handbag. Plucking her leather cigarette case from the depths of the large bag, she turned back to Bette. "In a word, hon, I've failed," she said steadily. She paused to light a cigarette, drawing the taste of it in deeply before, indicating the thin cylinder between her fingers, she sighed. "I really can't afford this habit. At the moment, I'm on my economic knees."

"You're broke?"

"Well," Vichy grimaced. "Let's say I'm very badly bent. I have a little money—damn little—saved, and I do have the holiday engagement. But, come the first of the year, I am going to have to get down to some serious job hunting."

"Then you really did mean what you said!" Bette exclaimed. "You've given up your dreams of a Grammy?"

"I've given up my dreams, period," Vichy replied flatly. "The clouds have completely dissolved around my head. I know now there'll be no fame, no fortune, no Grammy."

"But, Vich—" Bette began in protest.

"No buts." Vichy cut her off with a sharp shake of her head. "I'm tired of it all—the piano bars, the dives, even the intimate little supper clubs, where no one is really ever listening." Her soft mouth twisted, as if with a sour taste. "I'm tired of men on the make who think I'm an easy

25

target. God"—her laugh rang hollow—"I'm just tired of men and their predictable lines and come-ons."

During the shocked silence that followed her outburst, Vichy crushed out her cigarette and immediately lit another.

"I'm sorry, hon," Vichy apologized softly. "I really had no intention of laying my grief in your lap." She hesitated, then laughed self-deprecatingly. "I guess what I was going to do was lay it in Mom's lap." She shrugged helplessly. "So much for the independent self-image I've been harboring."

"You really are tired of it all, aren't you?" Bette's face mirrored her concern.

"Yes." A genuine smile restored Vichy's lips to their natural, sweet line. "I'm somewhat like a runaway teenager in reverse. Instead of running away from home, I'm running back to it."

At that moment the back door opened and the one voice Vichy had been longing most to hear exclaimed: "Victoria Lynn Parks, why didn't you let us know you were coming home? Dad and I would not have left the house for a second if we'd known."

CHAPTER TWO

Long after the voices of today had grown silent, Vichy lay in her bed listening to the voices of yesterday.

"Hurry up, slowpoke. You don't want to be late for your first day at school, do you?" The fourteen-year-old Mattie had chided her six-year-old self, right in this very room.

"Hey, bones," a ten-year-old Josh had called up the stairs to a thin, seven-year-old Vichy—then Vicky. "Your giggly girl friend Sue is on the phone."

"Is Mommy going to die?" Vichy's eight-year-old, tearful voice asked fearfully.

"Of course not, pumpkin." The maturing voice of the then-sixteen-year-old Mattie assured. "Mommy will be home before you know it with a brand new brother or sister for us."

"Vic-key."

"Vich-ee."

"Vic-key."

"Vich-ee."

"No, no, Bette, it's like this," the fourteen-and-a-half-year-old Josh pleaded with his eighteen-month-old baby sister.

"Vic-key. Now you say that."

"Vich-ee." Everyone smiled at baby Bette's effort.

"Okay," Josh had figuratively thrown up his hands. "You win, bright eyes, Vichy it is."

And Vichy it had remained.

"Silly fool."

The words were whispered into the dark room through quivering lips. Blinking against the hot sting flooding her eyes, Vichy sat up and clasped her arms around her raised knees. All of a sudden she wanted, very badly, to hug Mattie and Josh close to her love-parched heart.

Yes, indeed, she thought wryly, rubbing her eyes against the comforter covering her knees, *you are one silly fool.* But, Lord, it was good to be home!

Tears sparkling in the shaft of moonlight that cast her bed in a pearllike light, Vichy went over the hours following her parents' return from the market.

The water works had burst from her first look at her small, plump mother, standing just inside the kitchen door, a produce-stuffed shopping bag in each hand.

The moisture had slipped from between her eyelids a second time when, on entering the house moments after his wife, her father had caught Vichy close in a fierce, emotion-revealing bear hug.

At her mother's insistence, they made a call to Mattie in Williamsport. Vichy smiled shakily as the echo of her sister's voice sang in her mind.

"You're home to stay," Mattie had cried in delight. "Oh, Vich, that's wonderful. I'll bet Mom and Dad are overjoyed. And, oh, yes, has Mom told you?" she rushed on. "I'm going to be a grandmother in April, and now you'll be here—we'll all be together again."

Now the memory of her sister's happy voice drew a fresh deluge of tears. Reaching for a tissue from the box on the nightstand by her bed, Vichy assimilated Mattie's news.

Little Nan, the first of her parents' grandchildren, pregnant! It seemed impossible, yet, Nan's wedding September a year ago had been the reason Vichy had made a quick visit home.

How beautiful they had looked, both the nineteen-year-old Nan and her seventeen-year-old sister, Brenda. Come to that, Vichy smiled in the darkness, Mattie had looked pretty darn beautiful herself at thirty-seven.

Vichy had no sooner said good-bye to Mattie than her mother was dialing Josh's number in Easton. Her brother's reaction to her news was no less enthusiastic then Mattie's had been.

"Hey, that's terrific," Josh had fairly shouted. "You've probably made Mom and Dad's day. Day, hell, you've probably made their year. I can't wait to tell Caroline."

Vichy chuckled in the still room, her amusement renewed at the memory of where Josh had told her his wife, Caroline, and his young son were. It was too much! Tears surrendered to laughter. Rotten Robert, the scourge of the family, in a dance class! Oh, that poor dance instructor.

In the end, Vichy had not laid her problems in her mother's lap, nor had she cried, figuratively or otherwise, on her mother's shoulder. Her parents had accepted, without questioning, her explanation of being tired of working at night.

That she had not fooled them for one minute Vichy was sure of. She was equally sure they would not pry or try to force the issue.

Sighing with contentment, Vichy slid back down under the covers. Her contentment was premature and short-lived. Eyes closed, composed for sleep, new voices intruded, shatteringly painful, even after six years.

"You have a beautiful body, made for love. There's nothing to be ashamed of. Let me love you, darling. I mean *really* love you."

How many times had Brad whispered those impassioned words within those short two weeks from the day they met until the day he'd slipped the ring on her finger? More times than Vichy cared to remember.

But, whether she cared to remember or not, the bittersweet memories flowed on. Eyes tightly closed, Vichy felt her cheeks flush as in her mind she lay in Brad's arms, innocently happy in the fulfillment of his physical lovemaking.

Defenseless in her love and trust, Vichy had made her handsome young husband the center of her existence, physically and emotionally. And for six months Brad had taken full advantage of that trust, gorging himself on her, coaching her on the ways and means of arousing and satisfying *him*.

At the end of those six months Brad had proved himself a rat. But, Lord, he had been a hot-blooded rat!

Vichy groaned aloud. She had found out, in a degrading and shocking way, precisely how hot-blooded and how very much of a rat Brad was, six months to the day of their wedding.

Moving restlessly under the suddenly oppressive, hand-made comforter, Vichy tried in vain to block the torrent of memories that should no longer have had the power to humiliate her, but did.

"You've become my life"—Brad had vowed fervently countless times during those months—"my only reason for existing." She had actually believed him.

His handsome face expressing tenderness, his hands gently caressing, Brad had bound her to him with his beguiling words.

"I need you every bit as much as I need air to breathe. No woman I've ever known has had the power to make me feel as complete as I feel with you."

There had been more, much, much more of the same. On and on, ad nauseam, Vichy remembered cynically. *And I swallowed the bait, hook, line, and sinker. But then,* Vichy exonerated herself, *I was so unbelievably innocent, and Brad was so very good at it that even a seasoned veteran could have been forgiven for eating up every one of his words.* But it was the last words he'd spoken to her that still stuck in her mind—festering, shaming her.

Giving up tiredly, Vichy allowed the memories free run, praying against hope that airing them would, at long last, expunge them.

Some four months after their marriage Brad's honey-tipped tongue had even soothed away the devastation Vichy felt on being informed, during a routine visit to a doctor, that she would probably never be able to conceive a child.

"We have each other," he had crooned. "And you have

31

your career." It was not until much later that Vichy was to wonder if his deep sigh had been one of disappointment or relief.

Vichy had considered it pure good luck when she had been booked into the same lounge, in the same hotel in which they'd met, at the time of their six months' anniversary. And even better luck that Brad had been able to secure the same room in which they had spent their wedding night.

Her engagement had called for two appearances a night, the first at dinnertime, the second later in the evening for the drinking crowd. Brad, a compulsive gambler who loved every minute of it, winning or losing, never appeared for the early show. But, every night for two short weeks, he would stroll into the room sometime during her last performance. Vichy always knew the exact moment he sauntered through the room, for wherever he went, female eyes followed his progress and lips murmured in appreciation of his passage.

Vichy had been only momentarily concerned the night he had not shown up at all. Only for a second had she considered looking through his favorite rooms for him, so sure had she been that he had planned some kind of six-month-anniversary surprise for her.

Wondering what form that surprise would take, excitement coursing through her, Vichy had hurried to their room.

Flinging herself onto her side, Vichy buried her face in her pillow to muffle the whimper of pity that escaped her lips for the shock her younger self had received on entering that hotel room.

Dupe that she had been, Vichy had not even wondered

why the door to their room was locked. Fingers trembling in anticipation, she had still somehow managed to insert the key, turn the lock, and open the door silently.

The room was bathed in a soft light from the lamp on the dresser, illuminating clearly the couple locked together on the bed. As if turned to stone, Vichy had frozen in place two steps inside the room, her mind trying to deny the scene her eyes were riveted to. But there was no denying the position of the man and the woman, nor any question of their identities. The woman was a cocktail waitress in the lounge Vichy was engaged in. The man was most definitely Brad. Her Brad!

They had been so totally involved with pleasuring each other that even now Vichy had no idea what had alerted them to her presence. Had she cried out or gasped aloud? Vichy didn't know, but, then, what difference did it make now?

Choking with revulsion, Vichy had backed away from the sight of his sensuous face, the sound of the woman's excited laughter. To this very day, Vichy was unclear as to exactly where she'd gone that night. In a town that never seemed to sleep, she had walked, sightlessly, until, becoming aware of the time somewhere around nine a.m., she had walked into a lawyer's office. Within those lone nighttime hours Vichy had grown up—the hard way.

Lessons learned painfully are never forgotten. Vichy had not forgotten, nor had she been able to love any man since. To her way of thinking, except for her father and brother, the male of the species were simply not to be trusted.

Cold fingers brushed away the tears pooling under her eyes. Vichy was not crying for the woman she was today, but for the starry-eyed innocent she'd been six years ago. The death of that innocence had been painful in the extreme. Rebuilding her life at twenty-three after she'd received her divorce, six months after she had seen the lawyer, had been plain hard work. Being aware of the fact that she was the first member of her family to obtain a divorce had not made the rebuilding any easier.

Oh, there had been men in her life over the years, several in fact. But she never let any of them get too close. That in itself had not been easy, for while she held them off, she fought a silent battle with herself.

Brad had awakened her sensual being, had created in her a natural hunger. She had all the normal needs and urges of a healthy young woman. Fear lent her the strength to repress those needs. She'd vowed that never again would she leave herself open to the type of crushing hurt Brad had inflicted on her. Momentary appeasement, she'd reasoned, was simply not worth the price.

But abstinence by choice demanded its own price, and after six years the coin of frustration and loneliness had become bloated by inflation, its emotional weight growing heavier each year.

Another groan whispered through her lips and Vichy kicked impatiently at the suddenly confining covers. *Perhaps I should take a lover,* she thought despairingly. *A stranger for the night, chosen coolly and coldbloodedly with one purpose only: relief and assuagement—my own.*

Soft bitter laughter lived only seconds in the dark room. After all these years she wouldn't know how to go about it. And, even if she did, she knew without doubt that she'd lack the courage to go through with it.

* * *

Two weeks of her mother's gentle, bustling care, her father's gruff protectiveness, and her sister's sometimes zany humor went a long way in filling the emptiness Vichy had felt yawning inside herself.

The first weekend she was home, Mattie, her husband, Tom, and their youngest daughter, Brenda, came to visit. Most of the first day was spent on Vichy and Mattie catching up on the news of each other. Talk filled the house, sometimes everyone talking at once. Vichy was given a glowing report on her pregnant niece's health, Mattie's excitement over becoming a grandmother evident in every word she spoke.

The second day found them settled into comfortable conversation, broken at intervals by the high-spirited banter between Bette and Brenda, who were separated in age by only four years.

The second weekend Josh descended on them, Robert in tow. During that weekend pandemonium ran rampant, and by the time Josh and Caroline departed for Easton with the scourge, Vichy was beginning to feel like the self she had once been.

All of which made it that much harder for Vichy to leave again to honor her commitment in Atlantic City. But, telling herself she had only two short runs to go, leave she did the weekend before Thanksgiving.

Atlantic City was hardly recognizable as the same city in which her whole family had vacationed the year Vichy was eight. Admittedly, Vichy's memory of that time was sketchy, yet, the change was so dramatic she could not possibly fail to notice.

Though the streets were jammed with cars and tour buses, the city itself had a forgotten, overlooked air about it, not unlike a faded beauty whose admirers and lovers have left her, alone and deserted. Just driving through it depressed Vichy, making her vaguely sad.

At the boardwalk it was an altogether different story. There the atmosphere bubbled and sparkled like champagne, and was just as heady.

Buses, cabs, and private cars disgorged passengers everywhere. Female laughter rose above the babble of voices, punctuated regularly by the shrill whistles of hotel doormen.

Vichy located the hotel she was to perform in without difficulty and, following the instructions she'd received, made her way through the throng of people inside to the designated office.

Vichy found the small lounge she was to sing in just that—small and intimate. After a brief consultation with the manager of the lounge, Vichy went to her room. A hot shower dispensed with most of the tension tightening the muscles at the back of her neck and her shoulders, caused by a combination of nearly three hours of driving plus the apprehension of walking cold into a new job.

The first set on Sunday went smoothly. It was at the beginning of the second set, as Vichy's eyes scanned the sparsely populated room, that her glance collided with the piercing one of a dark-haired man sitting alone at a front table.

After ten years of performing in rooms very much like this one, Vichy was not unused to being stared at, but there was something about this man's riveting gaze that made her uneasy.

Time and again, while she went through her numbers, as if being compelled by a force too strong to deny, Vichy found her glance straying back to the man. And each time, for the length of a sigh, her glance was caught by his steady stare.

His face, rather harshly chiseled, even in composure, wore no expression. Did he hate the sound of her voice? Did he enjoy it? Vichy could not tell, for he didn't smile, he didn't frown. He just sat there, regarding her with that cool, unsettling, straight-on stare.

By the time Vichy had finished for the night and made her hasty retreat to her room, she had decided that if, for whatever reason, the man's goal had been to rattle her, he had achieved his purpose; she was thoroughly unnerved. If his desire had been to make her aware of him, in that he had also succeeded; she had hardly been aware of anyone else in the lounge.

Her dreams that night were peppered with an unsmiling countenance that stared numerous holes right through her.

When she began her last set on Monday night, she was almost afraid to scan the room. She had not seen even a hint of him during her earlier sets, but . . . Telling herself to grow up, Vichy launched herself into a popular, upbeat song, her eyes beginning a slow perusal of the scattered faces fanned before her. At the opposite side of the room from where she'd begun, her gaze came to a jolting stop. He was back!

Fighting a sudden, inexplicable urge to run for cover, Vichy, a hard-fought-for smile cracking her face, plodded through her repertoire, her glance dancing to encompass the room—except for one spot.

As the last note of her final number faded away, Vichy began a slow circuit of the room, pausing to greet the customers, bestow a smile, and murmur a soft "thank you" if complimented.

Studiously avoiding the section of the room where her tormenter sat, Vichy smilingly turned away from a young couple near the back of the lounge to find her way blocked by the very person she'd so carefully tried to steer clear of. His words were as direct as his staring eyes had been.

"You have a very sexy voice," he said softly. "But, of course, you know that."

Before Vichy could even begin to form a reply, he murmured an invitation that sounded more like a command.

"Come have a drink with me." His harshly cast features relaxed with a spine-tingling smile. "Let me flatter you into having a late supper with me."

Without waiting for an answer, in fact while he was still speaking, he curled long, slender fingers around her arm and began leading her in the direction of the table he'd occupied.

Bemused by the startling change his smile made to his visage, Vichy moved dazedly, allowing him to not only draw her with him, but seat her at the table as well! Her wits returned as he seated himself opposite her.

"Look, Mr.—" Vichy hesitated, eyebrows arched questioningly.

"Larkin," he supplied quietly. "Bennett Larkin."

"Look, Mr. Larkin," Vichy began again. "Thank you for your offer, but—" She got no further, for he cut in smoothly.

"Surely you eat?" The corners of his beautifully sculptured if somewhat thin lips twitched with the beginnings of another smile.

"Yes, of course, but—" she began again, only to have him cut in once more.

"Well, then, why not eat with me?" he queried, his tone mild.

"I don't even know you!" Vichy exclaimed softly.

"Not yet," he parried. "That's the point in having supper together."

"Mr. Larkin, I—" Vichy paused, her mind searching for polite words of refusal; after all, one did not antagonize the paying customers.

"Ben," he said softly.

"What?" The very softness of his tone had been lost to the muted murmurs of the other patrons. His tone rose half a notch.

"I said, my name is Ben."

"Yes, well"—Vichy swallowed against her strangely parched throat—"I'm sorry, but—"

"Have you a date for supper?" he rapped in a suddenly rough tone.

"No!" Vichy denied it at once, then chided herself for not ending the matter by giving an unqualified yes.

"There you are, then." His tone lifted with the corners of his mouth. "Why should we both eat alone, when we can keep each other company?"

CHAPTER THREE

Why indeed? Vichy wondered. If she was honest with herself, she had to admit that she was tired of constantly being alone.

It was strange, she mused, regarding Bennett Larkin from behind the barrier of self-imposed detachment, considering how many years she'd been, for the most part, alone. She had made friends, of course, but all of her relationships had been of the surface, casual type. Except for Brad, whom she refused to even count.

Why, now, had these past few days on her own seemed so barren? Very likely, she concluded, because of the fullness of her days during the two weeks she'd spent at home, with her family around her.

"Was the question too difficult?" Bennett Larkin's somewhat sardonic tone demanded she sit up and pay attention.

"What? Oh, I'm sorry, but where were you thinking of having supper?" Vichy hedged.

"Wherever," he shrugged. "Does it matter?"

"No, uh, I suppose not," Vichy finally answered.

"We could eat in one of the rooms right here," he waved his hand languidly to encompass the building. "Or," he paused, then asked, "are you hungry? I mean really hungry?"

"Well," Vichy hesitated, then answered honestly, "yes, as a matter of fact, I am." She had not rested well the night before, then had compounded the resultant edginess by pouring cup after cup of coffee into her tired body. At this moment she suffered from three afflictions—nervousness, hunger, and an unsettling sense of lonesomeness.

"There's a Japanese restaurant not far from here." He mentioned one of the casino hotels. "For a set price they serve a seven-course meal. There is no mulling, or indecision, over a menu. The majority of the food is prepared in front of you, on a grill set into the table, by a very dexterous chef. The meal is served in a courteous, leisurely manner. Does the idea appeal to you?" he finished quietly.

"Very much," Vichy admitted.

"Then why are we sitting here?" Rising abruptly, he came to help her out of her chair, not exactly rushing her, but giving her no time to change her mind either.

"I must get a coat," Vichy said as Ben started toward the steps that led out of the lounge.

"All right." He gave her a measuring glance, then added, "While you do that, I'll call ahead to make sure they can accommodate us." Again that measuring glance swept over her. "If you want to meet me at the lobby entrance, I'll have a cab waiting."

"Couldn't we walk?" Vichy asked, feeling the need of some exercise outdoors.

"Certainly, if you prefer," he concurred at once. "A stroll in the sea air might sharpen the appetite. I'll meet you at the boardwalk exit."

When she went for her coat, Vichy caught a glance of herself in the mirror and decided she'd better remove her stage makeup if she didn't want to be stared at like some sideshow freak. Aware of the minutes slipping by, and of Bennett Larkin waiting, she worked swiftly, but carefully, creaming the heavier makeup off and applying a lighter coat more suitable for being seen in public. And all the time she worked, she tried to avoid thinking about the fact that she had just made a date to have dinner with a perfect stranger.

As she approached the appointed exit, Vichy spied Bennett Larkin before he saw her and used the short interval to study him.

In the dimly lighted lounge, his hair had simply appeared to be dark brown, much like her own. But in the well-lit area before the exit doors, Vichy could see his hair was actually a deep shade of auburn, the red highlights gleaming in the artificial illumination. He was taller than most of the men that passed him going in and out, and his shoulders were wide, his chest broad. His well-cut, perfectly fitted suit revealed a narrow waist, slim hips, and long legs. His arms hung limply at his sides, the fingers of one hand snapping impatiently, belying his relaxed stance.

In the darkened lounge his face had seemed somewhat harsh. Now, in the light, his features appeared chiseled, the cheekbones high, the nose almost hawkish, the jaw jutting out aggressively.

The well-shaped head turned, his eyes sweeping over the faces of the people in front of her before fastening onto her own. Suppressing a shiver, Vichy forced a small smile, asking herself: *What am I doing?* His expression was so fierce it actually frightened her.

"I was beginning to think you weren't going to show," he murmured as she walked up to him. "Did you have to fight second thoughts?" Vichy did not care for his tone or his fierce look. What was she getting into here? she asked herself nervously. His tone had had an underlying note of possession that sent a chill of warning down her spine. Should she try and beg off? she wondered. Would he give her an argument if she did? The answer came without hesitation. Yes, he would. Vichy didn't know quite how she knew, but she did.

"No," she answered simply. "I'm sorry I kept you waiting. I had to remove my stage makeup." Vichy had never before seen eyes the color of the ones studying her now. His eyes were brown, yes, but they actually had deep red flecks in them. Were these what she had heard referred to as sherry-colored? Giving an imperceptible shrug of her shoulders, she preceded him through the door he held open for her.

After the warmth of the smoky lounge, the sharp salt air had an invigorating effect. Sliding her hands into the slash pockets of her all-weather coat, Vichy walked beside Ben, only vaguely aware of the clacking sound her heels made on the almost-deserted boardwalk.

"Are you tired, or are you always this quiet?" Bennett Larkin angled his head, slanting her a questioning glance.

Vichy swallowed against the sudden odd something tightening her throat. "I am a little tired, but, yes, I'm

43

usually this quiet." *Comes from being alone so much,* she could have added, but didn't.

"That's a relief," he drawled. "I was beginning to think my company had stifled your power of speech."

Glancing at him quickly, Vichy caught a flickering, sardonic curve that touched his lips.

"It's a rare quality in women, quietness," he went on softly. "Most of the females I know chatter incessantly, usually about nothing of any importance."

"Importance to whom?" Vichy couldn't resist the small dig. Why did men always think that the topics that concerned them were important?

"Ah, she's quiet, but she does have claws." A note of satisfaction underlined his smooth tone.

"Oh, yes," Vichy warned lightly. "She does have claws. Teeth too."

"Indeed?" His sherry eyes lit from within. "Very intriguing. I'll keep it in mind."

Something in his tone sent a tingle sliding down her spine and started a small fluttering in her midsection. *Careful, Vichy, this one knows his way around the distaff side.* At that moment they reached the hotel, relieving her of her fruitless search for an effective retort.

On their arrival at the restaurant they were seated at once by a pleasant, soft-spoken maître d'. The table was rectangular and set for eight, the place settings arranged on three sides around a large grill.

A young couple, so obviously in love that Vichy wondered if they were on their honeymoon, were already seated at the table. They glanced up curiously, and Ben extended his hand to the young man.

"Bennett Larkin," he informed quietly. "And this is

44

Victoria Parks." He recited the name that was on the lounge's advertisement board.

"Kevin and Donna Wheatley," the young man smiled before turning his attention back to his pretty wife.

"Honeymooners," Ben murmured, echoing her own thoughts.

Although their drink order was taken and quickly brought, the meal was not begun until the table had a full complement of eight, which consisted of an elderly couple and two women Vichy judged to be somewhere between forty and forty-five.

As Ben had informed Vichy, most of the meal was prepared on the grill before them by a charming young man. The rest of the meal—the sake and a clear, green tea—was served by a lovely, whispery-voiced young woman, who looked like a delicate Japanese doll in a colorful kimono.

During the course of the meal, and the ensuing conversation around the table, Vichy learned that the young couple were on their wedding trip, that the two women were on a one-day bus tour, that the elderly couple had stopped off in Atlantic City on their way from New Hampshire to Florida on a driving trip, and, most important to Vichy, that Bennett Larkin was in the city for one reason—to gamble.

Vichy had, of course, suspected as much, but having him so casually confirm her suspicions tightened nerves that the comfortable atmosphere had just begun to relax. But that didn't mean that gambling was his life, Vichy reminded herself. Oh, why was she trying to make excuses for this man, she wondered then, when he could very well be Brad all over again?

After bidding their table companions good night, Vichy and Ben left the restaurant.

"Do you want to take a cab or walk back?" Ben asked as they rode the escalator to the ground floor.

"After all that food, I think I'd better walk," Vichy smiled. "I can't remember ever eating so much in one sitting."

Holding her coat for her at the exit doors, Ben's eyes ran over her figure consideringly.

"It would appear to me that you have been eating hardly anything at all at any one sitting," he observed dryly.

"Is that a roundabout way of telling me I'm too skinny?" she demanded. Vichy was more than a little touchy on the subject of her weight, or lack of it, having been chided about it by every member of her family at least once over the two weeks she'd been at home.

"Not at all," he denied smoothly. "More a roundabout way of giving a compliment. Your figure is just about perfect, at least for my taste it is."

Vichy's pulses leaped erratically, startling her. After all these years performing in front of the public, she was used to compliments, honestly given or not. Why should this stranger's offhand remark have the power to fluster her? And there was no denying to herself that she was flustered. It was weird. She didn't care what this man thought of her figure or anything else. Did she?

Her shoulder being jostled made Vichy realize that they were still standing in front of the exit doors, hindering traffic. Bennett Larkin's amused expression made her uncomfortably aware of the fact that he knew of her confused state and was enjoying every minute of it.

With a stiltedly murmured "thank you," Vichy swept

past him out onto the boardwalk. Without pausing to see if he was beside her, she started walking as fast as her heels would allow.

"What's the rush?"

His fingers curled around her arm, halting her headlong pace, before sliding slowly down to capture, and entwine with, hers.

Vichy opened her mouth, then closed it again, shocked speechless by the riot of sensations radiating from her imprisoned hand all the way up her arm to her shoulder.

"It's very late," she began. His soft laughter stopped the rest of whatever she was going to say in her mouth. Good Lord! What was happening to her? Vichy could not remember feeling this way while in the company of a man since . . . No! She would *not* think about Brad. She tried to disentangle her hand, but Ben's fingers tightened around hers.

"Don't panic, beautiful," Ben advised softly, close to her ear. "I'm not going to make any sudden overt moves or shocking suggestions." He shook her hand slightly. "I'm not going to let go either. Enjoy our stroll," he urged, "and this perfect fall night." His tone went very low. "Relax and let nature take its course."

Vichy had a very good idea exactly which course he referred to. The very thing she'd been so carefully avoiding all these years. A shiver of—of apprehension or anticipation?—rippled through her body. Bennett Larkin felt it, of course.

"For God's sake, woman," he growled impatiently, "ease up." He came to a complete stop and turned to face her, his expression baffled. "You're as nervous and uptight

47

as a teenager on her first date. But, as you are very obviously *not* a teenager, what's your problem, anyway?"

Vichy stiffened at his exasperated tone. Who did this guy think he was? And did he think that buying her supper gave him the right to question her? Or make remarks about her age and attitude? And she didn't like being called "woman" either! Once again she tried to pull her hand from his—and failed.

"Let go of my hand, please." Vichy was proud of the cool tone she'd managed.

"No." His tone held flat finality. "Answer me."

His implacability shattered most of her cool. "You're right," she snapped. "I'm far from being a teenager. I have been around, as the saying goes. If I have a problem, it is men, like you, who take entirely too much for granted. Now, let go of my hand—and don't call me 'woman.'"

"My, my, you're even more uptight than I thought," Ben marveled infuriatingly. "Some jerk rake you over the coals, did he?"

"That is none of your business," Vichy ground out through clenched teeth.

"True," he agreed easily, which incensed her even more. "But that doesn't stop me from wondering what he did to you."

"You can wonder until the cows come home," she spat out angrily. "I have no intention of pandering to your curiosity." Again she tried, and failed, to disengage her hand. "And if you don't mind"—she gave another unsuccessful tug against his grip—"I'm tired, I want to go to my room."

"Okay," he sighed deeply, exaggeratedly. Without warning he began to walk, tugging her along.

An uneasy silence hung between them like a tangible presence all the way back. A silence that went unbroken until, standing before the door to her room, his hand covered hers as she attempted to insert her key into the lock.

"Victoria, wait," Ben urged softly. His other hand came up to grasp her shoulder and turn her to face him. His somewhat austere features betrayed confusion. "I'm damned if I can figure out why what I said upset you. But, as it obviously did, I'm sorry. If I promise to ask no more personal questions, will you have supper with me again tomorrow night?"

Vichy's pulse leaped. Good grief, she chided herself in confusion, hadn't she just gone out of her way to discourage him? She knew that if she had any sense at all she'd say no.

"Yes." So much for sense.

"Good." His warm breath feathered her forehead as he lowered his head.

He was going to kiss her, she knew it, and yet she stood, unable to move, her eyes fastened on his firmly outlined mouth as it drew closer to her own.

"Ben!"

Her whispered protest was too late. His mouth touched her parted lips for gentle seconds, and then he lifted his head and stepped back. His fingers plucked the key from hers and a moment later the door swung inward, the keychain dangling from the lock.

"Good night, Victoria."

Leaning to her, he lightly brushed his lips across her cheek, and then he was gone, striding down the hallway.

Jerking like someone coming out of a trance, Vichy

hurried into the room, closed and locked the door, then, breathing deeply, leaned back against the wood panels weakly.

What is it about this man? she asked herself blankly. Her chest felt constricted and she had a strangely hollow feeling inside.

Shaking her head sharply, Vichy pushed herself away from the door. No, she was overreacting, she assured herself bracingly. She was attracted to him, yes, but it was purely a physical attraction, nothing more. Surely she could handle that.

As she moved around the small room preparing for bed, Vichy rationalized her totally out-of-character response to Bennett Larkin. Never before had she gone off with a complete stranger as she had tonight. Hadn't she even kept Brad at arm's length for several days after they'd been introduced before agreeing to go out with him? But, she was so childishly homesick and lonely, much more so than she'd been at twenty-two. Then she'd had the fullness of the promise of the future to combat the occasional pangs of emptiness. Bennett Larkin had lit the first spark of life in her in what seemed like ages.

On the verge of sliding into bed, Vichy went still with a cautioning thought: *Be very careful, Vichy Parks, that the spark Ben Larkin fired doesn't flare into a full-blown blaze. You've been burned before; play it cool.*

After settling herself for sleep, Vichy deliberately conjured up a mental picture of Ben Larkin, again asking herself, *What is it about him?*

She had met so many men over the years, some of them almost unbelievably handsome that, comparatively, Ben was merely very attractive, and that in a harshly masculine way. A tiny, live wire of excitement shot through her body. Was that it? Was it that raw masculinity about him that appealed to something within her? Vichy shivered. She knew nothing about him but one thing—he was all male.

Vichy's last thought before drifting off to sleep was, all male or not, he's a gambler, and not to be trusted—or was he?

CHAPTER FOUR

Tuesday was much like Monday, except for one major difference—all day long thoughts of Ben stole into Vichy's mind, bringing with them a mixture of excitement and trepidation.

Periodically swinging from feeling breathless to foolish, even she heard the new nerve in her voice as she sang her way through her first performance.

Touching up her makeup before her final set, Vichy couldn't help but notice the flush of color in her cheeks. Stroking a brush through her mane of dark hair, she studied her appearance critically. Her dress had cost a great deal, and it was worth every penny. In a pale lilac, the soft silk material clung to her full breasts and small waist, then swirled out enticingly around her slender calves.

Finally satisfied with the smooth shine of her hair, Vichy stowed the brush in her bag, wet her lips with the tip of her tongue, and, swallowing to relieve a sudden tickle in her throat, went back to work.

A quick inspection of the lounge left her feeling as flat as a bottle of uncorked, week-old champagne. Ben wasn't there!

Never missing a beat, or forgetting a word, Vichy sang, talked to the audience, and laughingly bantered with the combo that backed her up musically, all the while upbraiding herself for the depth of disappointment she was experiencing. He was a gambler. Hadn't she learned the hard way that gamblers could not be trusted? But the same nagging thought she had tried to push out of her mind kept coming back. Maybe he was different, maybe she had misjudged him. . . .

The set seemed endless. Lord, had she really rehearsed all these numbers? At last, only one more song to go! Then she could go back to her room and cry, or throw something, or curse all gamblers out loud.

Flashing her listeners a brilliant smile, Vichy opened her mouth and very nearly missed the first note. Moving casually and looking extremely attractive, Ben Larkin made his way to the table he'd sat at the previous two nights.

Felling her anger in its path, joy welled up inside and voiced itself through her music, drawing from the audience the most enthusiastic round of applause she'd received since beginning her engagement. Ben was equally appreciative.

"I'm doubly sorry now that I arrived so late." The smile that revealed his even, white teeth sent an expectant chill along her spine. "I fear I've missed a very exciting performance."

Lackluster, Vichy silently corrected him while aloud she murmured, "Thank you," and returned his smile.

"Don't sit down." Ben took her arm as she made a move to do just that. "I've had the car brought around. Go take your makeup off as quickly as possible."

"But—"

"Go," he ordered gently. "We wouldn't want the doorman unhappy with us. The car's taking up space."

Vichy removed her makeup in record time. Carrying her coat, she went back to him and, without a word, he ushered her to the lobby and out of the building. Slipping a bill to the uniformed doorman, Ben led her toward a sleek-looking black Grand Prix. Allowing the doorman to seat her, he strode around to the driver's side and slid behind the wheel. Vichy remained quiet until they were through the worst of the congested traffic and headed away from the city. Now, after being tense and jumpy all day, a sense of contentment enfolded her like a warm pair of arms.

"At the risk of sounding nosy," she taunted lightly, "might I be permitted to ask where we're going?"

At her easy, teasing tone, Ben shifted his eyes from the road to her face in a swift, encompassing glance. His slow smile carried the impact of a sledgehammer.

"Feel good, do you?" he teased back, his sherry eyes lit from within. "We're going to have supper at a steak house along the road, several miles inland." He went on without waiting for a reply from her. "Does that meet with your approval?"

Vichy's soft laughter was a clear indication of her suddenly light-hearted mood. "Would it matter terribly if it didn't?"

"Terribly," he intoned with mock seriousness. "I'd be devastated."

"I think you're pulling my leg," she accused laughingly.

"Oh, no," Ben drawled, slicing her a glinting look. "If I ever pull on your leg, beautiful, you won't have to think about it—you'll know."

His tone as well as the innuendo sent a shaft of warmth radiating through her body and Vichy was grateful for the darkness that concealed her flushed cheeks from him.

Whatever had come over her? she wondered, studying his relaxed profile from under lowered lashes. If any other man had made that remark to her in just that suggestive tone, she'd have withdrawn behind a wall of ice. *What is it about this man?* Vichy asked herself for at least the hundredth time. *Why does he have the power to reduce me to a blushing inarticulateness?* He was only a man, and probably a gambler at that. If she had any sense at all, she would not even be here now.

"Am I receiving that silent treatment for being brash?" Ben's quiet taunt jerked her out of her introspection.

"Was I expected to respond to that crack?" Vichy parried.

"Crack?" Ben laughed aloud. "Oh, sweetheart, that was no crack. That was a promise."

Now, how in the world was she supposed to respond to *that?* Thankfully, she was spared the effort, as at that moment Ben brought the car to a near stop, then, his long hands controlling the wheel easily, he drove off the road into the parking lot of a long, single-story building which boasted a neon sign that proclaimed it a steak house.

Very likely due to the fact that it was a Tuesday night and fairly late, there were only a few patrons in the large, dimly lit dining room. They were greeted at the door by a smiling hostess, smartly dressed in a straight long black skirt and a crisp, long-sleeved white blouse. She escorted them to a secluded corner table, asked if they'd like to order a drink, then, after presenting overlarge menus for their perusal, went gliding away to place their drink order.

"That is a very classy-looking woman," Ben opined, his eyes following the swaying, retreating form.

"Yes," Vichy agreed tightly, appalled at the flash of annoyance his attention to the woman's appearance generated in her.

"But she can't hold a candle to you," he added teasingly, obviously not missing the strained note in her tone. His eyes dancing with devilment, he examined her face and the upper part of her body, lingering long seconds on her silk-draped, suddenly quivering breasts.

"Ben, s-stop it," Vichy pleaded constrictedly, glancing around nervously.

"Why?" Leaning back lazily, he raised gleaming eyes to hers. "Are you wearing a bra?" he asked softly, outrageously, chuckling softly at her quick gasp.

"That's none of your—" she began in a strangled groan, only to gasp again at his soft laughter.

"I don't believe you are," he laughed, his eyes betraying the amusement he felt at bringing a rush of pink to her pale cheeks. "Of course," he drawled consideringly, "to be absolutely sure, I'll have to play the intrepid explorer— later on."

"You'll do nothing of the kind!" Vichy exclaimed in another shocked gasp.

56

Ben's delighted laughter bounced around the nearly empty room, drawing the eyes and smiles of patrons and staff alike.

"Oh, Victoria, you're an absolute gem," Ben teased around the laughter that still rumbled in his muscled chest. "You snap at the bait like a starved fish."

"Better be careful," Vichy teased, falling under his playful spell. "You could find you've hooked a barracuda, with very tiny, but pointed, teeth."

"Ah, ha," he shot back. "But the barracuda is no match for the shark, who has very *large,* pointed teeth." His voice dropped to a low growl. "And this shark is already tempted to gobble up the barracuda." His eyes raked her like a rough caress. "And this particular barracuda is a very tasty-looking morsel indeed."

Catching sight of a waiter approaching their table, Vichy purred, "Luckily, this particular fish is about to have her scaly skin saved by a fisherman in the disguise of a waiter." She fluttered her long eyelashes innocently. "Are you going to order a barracuda steak?"

"Barbs like that only make the shark hungrier," Ben managed to jibe softly before the waiter came to a halt beside Vichy.

Suddenly famished, Vichy ordered a full-course dinner, from soup through dessert, and ate every bit of it. In between her first spoonful of broccoli-cheese soup and her last forkful of pecan pie, the conversation flowed easily between them.

"Victoria is such a straightlaced sort of name," Ben mused around his own spoonful of the rich soup. "Haven't you ever been called Vicky, or even Vic?"

"Vichy," she supplied.

57

"What?"

"Vich-ee," she repeated distinctly, shrugging lightly. "I have a sister eight years my junior. When she began to talk, she could not articulate Vicky. It always came out Vichy. The name stuck, even after she could have pronounced it correctly."

"I'm glad," Ben decided, after munching and swallowing a piece of his filet mignon. "It's different, like you."

"How am I different?" Vichy asked, glancing up from her plate in surprise.

"In many ways," Ben smiled. "I'll tell you sometime."

"Sometime?" Vichy echoed. "Why not now?"

Ben glanced around the room, empty now except for the employees. "Too public," he was teasing again. "You'll have to remind me to tell you when we have a little more privacy."

"Were you always a tormentor?" Vichy chided. "Even as a little boy?" Before he could answer, she tacked on, *"Were* you ever a little boy?" finding it hard to picture him any way but the way he was this minute.

"Of course I was a little boy once." His tone held effrontery. "I was even a baby at one time."

"Really?" Vichy breathed, wide-eyed.

His eyes glittered back at her.

"Had you thought that, perhaps, my parents had found me, fully grown, under a large boulder somewhere?"

"Natural offspring of a rock, you mean?" Vichy queried sweetly.

"I'm as hard as one," Ben's grin held wickedness. "Better be careful you don't bruise yourself against me."

The mere idea of being against him was enough to

fluster Vichy all out of proportion, and sidestepping, she stammered, "Have you, ah, any brothers or sisters?"

"Coward," he mocked, then with lifted brows and bland face asked, "Sibling stones, so to speak?"

"If you will," she laughed helplessly.

"Oh, I will," he taunted, deliberately twisting her meaning. "I will, *anything.*"

"Ben, be serious," Vichy admonished.

"I'm very serious," he answered her. "There are a number of things I will, with you—eventually. And that's another promise."

"Ben, please," Vichy begged, her dinner forgotten for the moment, lost, as she suddenly was, inside his sherry eyes. Those eyes, she decided vaguely, could be positively intoxicating.

"Is the barracuda ready to concede the battle?"

"Not on your fishhook," Vichy retorted.

"Just hiding out in the shallows, eh?" he wondered aloud. "Okay," he almost crooned. "I'll cut bait for a while." He speared a french fry, his eyes laughing at her. "I have one brother, no sisters." Popping the slice of potato into his mouth, he showed his teeth in a grin. "He's younger, not quite as hard as I am."

"Does he gamble too?" Vichy was sorry the moment the harsh-sounding words were out of her mouth, for Ben frowned, and the light in his eyes dimmed. His expression quizzical, he stared at her a long time before answering with a question of his own.

"Doesn't everyone?"

"Of course not!" Vichy exclaimed. "I don't."

"I think they do," Ben stated adamantly. "Yourself included."

"No," Vichy shook her head in denial. "I never—"

"Forget it," he interrupted brusquely. "I never argue over a meal." The light went on in his eyes again, and he smiled meltingly. "It's bad for the digestion, you know."

"But, Ben—" That's as far as she got, for Ben again cut determinedly across her attempt at protest.

"You mentioned a younger sister. Are there any others?"

"One other sister and a brother," Vichy sighed in defeat. "Both older than I."

"And is there a husband waiting at home?" he asked overly casually.

"No." Vichy kept her tone every bit as casual. "Is there a wife?"

"Not anymore," Ben declared grimly. His tone sent her eyebrows up in question. With a shrug, Ben clarified, "I've been divorced for three years."

"I've got three years on you." Her flat statement sent his brows arching. Emulating his careless shrug, Vichy explained, "It's been six years since I received my divorce decree."

"You must have been very young." It was a deliberate probe to ascertain her age, and Vichy knew it. She smiled wryly.

"I was twenty-three."

"I was thirty-one," Ben offered her the knowledge of his own age. "It's a bad experience at any age."

"Yes," Vichy nodded soberly.

"Were there any children?" he probed further.

"No." *Thank God,* she added silently. "You?" she sank her own probe.

"One, a boy." Ben's expression was suddenly so fierce

60

Vichy felt chilled with apprehension. The feeling deepened when he went on harshly. "I have custody."

Good Lord! A shiver slithered down Vichy's spine. He was frightening. His chiseled features had set into granite hardness. This would be the wrong man to cross, Vichy thought nervously. At that moment, without knowing any of the facts concerning the affair, Vichy felt compassion for his former wife.

"Chad's seven."

Ben's quietly voiced statement scattered Vichy's thoughts. Glancing at him quickly, she tried to discern his mood. A sigh of relief whispered through her lips. His expression had softened a little—and the gleam was back in his eyes.

"And is he as hard as you are?" she blurted out before she could stop herself.

"Not yet," he laughed without humor. "But he will be." His laughter subsided into a bitter smile. "No woman is ever going to rake him over the coals. I intend to see that he goes into the world fully prepared."

"To do the raking, instead of being raked?" Vichy asked bitingly.

"Bad, was it?" Ben queried softly.

"Very," Vichy clipped, revealing her impatience with him.

"Okay." He held up his hands in surrender. "Point taken. But, in my own defense, I must say that I have been instructing him on the proper way to treat a—a lady."

His deliberate pause was not lost on Vichy. *Holy cow,* Vichy thought wildly, *was he also instructing him on the proper way to treat a non-lady?* A second shiver followed the first one down her spine. Ben saw her involuntary movement.

"Something bothers you?"

Vichy smiled uncertainly. "I suddenly find myself hoping you consider me a lady."

Amusement twitching his lips, Ben lifted his stemmed wineglass that still contained an inch of the ruby burgundy he'd ordered, and tilted it toward her.

"A very special lady," he murmured assuringly.

By mutual if silent agreement, their conversation was kept to generalities for the remainder of the meal.

Over coffee and liqueur Ben broke the tacit agreement to remain impersonal. Raising his tiny glass, he studied its contents for a moment before, glancing up at her, he touched his glass to hers. He took a sip, then waited, brows arched, until she had followed suit. Vichy nearly choked with his murmured words.

"Amaretto, the drink of lovers." His smile invited—all kinds of things. "And we will be. That's another promise."

"Don't bet on it, gambler," Vichy advised angrily. She was furious, yet, underneath that fury, excitement sizzled, scaring her.

"I am betting on it," Ben said imperturbably. "Heavily."

"Ben—"

"Drink your coffee." His eyes roamed over the deserted room. "I think the hostess is trying to tell us something. She's positively glaring at us."

It was raining when they left the restaurant, not a downpour, but a steady rain Vichy's father would have called a land rain.

"I like to ride in the rain," Vichy announced after they

had settled into the car. "But I hate driving in it." She shuddered, remembering the deluge she'd struggled through on her way east.

"Well, sit back and enjoy it," Ben invited expansively. "I don't mind driving through it."

Made drowsy by all the food she'd consumed, Vichy dismissed the uneasiness Ben's last promise had aroused and snuggled into the velour upholstery. Assuring herself he could do nothing about fulfilling his outrageous promise without her compliance, she closed her eyes and allowed herself to be lulled by the swish of the windshield wipers.

"Vichy."

Ben's soft, gentle tone roused her out of a half-sleep. Sitting up quickly, Vichy blinked against the glare of light illuminating the hotel forecourt.

"I'm sorry, Ben." Vichy had to pause to smother a yawn behind her hand. "I'm not used to so much food at such a late hour. It sends me right to sleep," she avowed, conveniently forgetting her wakefulness of the night before.

"Apology accepted," Ben smiled warmly, "but entirely unnecessary. You work hard, you get tired. You owe no one an apology for that." He hesitated, then underlined darkly, confusingly, "Most especially me."

The ensuing activity of leaving the car prevented Vichy from inquiring into his meaning. But why him especially? she asked herself, wondering. She put the question to him as he escorted her to her room.

"Why, because I've witnessed the amount of energy you put into each performance," Ben explained glibly. But, as the seconds of quiet lengthened, Vichy had no option but to accept his answer at face value. Shrugging off the certainty that he was being less than truthful, Vichy let the matter rest.

As they approached her room, Vichy slipped her key from her purse to have ready in case she had to make a quick escape. Her forethought was wasted, for Ben, aware of her every move, simply took the key from her fingers and unlocked the door, allowing it to swing open before turning to face her with mocking eyes.

"Are you going to offer your mouth?" he taunted. "Or must I play the kiss thief again?"

"Ben, I—"

"Okay," he sighed deeply. "Have it your way." All the harsh angles and planes of his face settled into iron determination as he lowered his head toward hers.

"But, if I have to steal it, I may as well make it worth the effort."

His lips touched hers and the effort he put forth was shattering. Never in her life had Vichy been kissed quite like Ben was kissing her now. There was no slow build-up to possession. His mouth attacked, devoured, vanquished. His tongue raked hungrily for every drop of sweetness. His arms crushed her softness into submission to the hardness of his body.

Knowing herself beaten before she could launch an offensive, Vichy surrendered to his superior forces. At her first sign of the white flag, Ben's tactics switched to a new field of battle.

Bringing into play every sensual weapon he possessed, he proceeded to annihilate her faintest hope of resistance.

His mouth moving, his tongue teasing, his hands restlessly caressing, he lit a spark that ignited a sexual explosion, the effects of which singed to life every inch of her quivering body.

Without thought, without caution, Vichy's arms circled his waist convulsively as she arched herself to him, moaning a protest when his mouth slid from hers.

"Vichy," he groaned, the tip of his tongue exploring the corner of her mouth before trailing across her cheek to her ear. "Do you know what you're doing to me?"

"Yes," she admitted. Held so very closely against him, she could hardly deny the evidence of his arousal.

"Then invite me into your room," he urged unsteadily. "I can't make love to you here."

Every one of Vichy's inflamed senses froze. What was she doing? Was she out of her mind? She was not that kind of woman, was she? Cold, shivering with reaction, she struggled to free herself.

"You can't make love to me anywhere," she cried in a strangled croak. "Ben, please," she begged. "I can't."

His arms dropped away from her and he stepped back, his face a study in disgust.

"Why did you respond like that?" he demanded coldly.

"I—I—" What could she say? How could she defend an action she didn't understand?

"Don't strain yourself," Ben almost snarled. In an abrupt movement he turned to walk away from her, but he didn't walk away, or even move, for long seconds.

Barely breathing, Vichy watched him, a soft sigh easing out of her when she saw the tautness in his back slowly relax. When he turned back to face her, all sign of his blazing anger was gone.

"I don't think I've ever wanted a woman quite as badly as I want you," he said softly. "Fair warning, Vichy. You

65

might as well know I intend having you—and soon." His eyes narrowed on her suddenly trembling, kiss-bruised lips, and he smiled. "You, beautiful, are every bit as aroused as I am. I'm not the only one who will have trouble getting to sleep." His smile taunted pitilessly. "I won't say good night, because we both know it won't be." With that he turned and walked away, his long stride widening the distance between them.

CHAPTER FIVE

Over three hours later Vichy ruefully acknowledged the truth of Ben's parting barb. It was not a good night; in fact, it was a very bad night.

Vichy ached in places that had not felt the stirring of life for a very long time. Her body throbbed with a demand for release, making rest impossible. Her mind darted around like an animal in a cage seeking sleep-inducing, tranquil thoughts in vain.

Her mouth still savored the taste of Ben, her skin still tingled from his touch, and her body still felt his imprint. And most discomforting of all was the realization that she wanted him with near desperation.

This is beyond sense, she thought wildly, in an effort to calm her churning emotions. Frantically, she sought excuses for her own out-of-character behavior. *I've been alone too long. I'm tired. I'm losing my mind.*

Nothing worked. Near dawn, exhausted both physically

and mentally, Vichy faced the unpalatable truth her mind had been dodging since Ben had walked away from her.

He had said he'd never wanted a woman as badly as he wanted her. Vichy knew what he meant, for the truth she'd been so studiously avoiding was that her own desire equaled his.

She had loved Brad with all her heart and mind and yet, not even at the zenith of their lovemaking, had he had the power to bring her to this degree of awareness of herself as well as of him. That Ben so very obviously possessed that power shook her to her foundations.

Vichy moaned and buried her face in the mangled bed pillow. There had been several altogether different types of men interested in her over the years—a constructional engineer, a successful businessman, a live-wire from the advertising field, even her agent had made a play for her attention. She had liked all of them, and in the case of the engineer and her agent, very much. Yet none of them had ever dented the barrier of reserve she'd erected around herself after Brad's betrayal.

Now, this stranger, another gambler, had, within a few minutes' embrace, not only dented that barrier but shattered it completely.

What was it, Vichy wondered despairingly, that drew her to this reckless type of man? Unconscious rebellion against her own protected, moralistic upbringing? An unrecognized urge deep within her to throw caution to the winds and either soar or crash with the careless toss of a pair of dice or the turn of a card? Latent idiocy?

Vichy did not know nor could she be sure that Ben was as obsessed with gambling as Brad had been. Her thoughts revolved unceasingly as the room emerged from blackness to pearl-gray predawn and no rational answer presented itself.

One thing she did know. She would have to be mad to get within fifty feet of him again. He could hurt her badly. And if she saw more of him, she would be inviting the pain, for one concrete truth stood boldly unsinged in the ashes of her burned-out thoughts. It had been hours since he'd taken his leave, and she still wanted him.

Against all reason, against all sensible judgment, she still ached to be enfolded in his strong arms, still yearned to be drawn close to his hard body, still hungered for the taste of his marauding mouth. And with that urgency still burning along her nerve endings and through her veins, Vichy finally slipped into a deep, dreamfree sleep.

Vichy had never been overwild about Wednesday, coming, as it did, in the middle of the week. It had always been *the* day to get through. Friday, she had always maintained, she could do standing on her head, but Wednesday was a drag. This particular Wednesday was worse than most.

Three hours of sleep definitely did not leave one bright of eye and dewy-skinned, Vichy concluded as she deftly camouflaged her face with cosmetics.

During the process of preparing herself to venture outside the relatively safe confines of her room, Vichy raked her mind as to how she was going to accomplish her objective of avoiding Bennett Larkin.

Lord, just thinking his name had the effect of a featherlight massage with icy fingers. Vichy shivered, and, repressing a sigh, examined the finished product of her labors in the mirror above the room's single dresser.

With blatant bravado, she had chosen a pair of narrow-legged, camel's hair wool slacks and topped them with a champagne-colored cashmere V-neck sweater. The thin, soft wool outlined her perfect figure. Chocolate brown leather high-heeled boots enhanced her long legs.

Even in a place where lovely women were the norm, eyes followed Vichy as she made her way to the coffee shop where she'd breakfasted every morning since her arrival at the hotel. As she sat in the same section each day, she invariably was served by the same waiter, and this morning he was quick to comment on her appearance.

"Morning, Ms. Parks." His bright young eyes made a detailed inventory of her entire person before he quipped, "You look good enough to be listed on the menu under desserts."

"Thank you," Vichy smilingly returned his boyish grin. "I think."

Even though the waiter was about her sister Bette's age, his obvious admiration bolstered her spirits and she left the coffee shop with a much lighter tread then when she'd entered.

Rehearsal, and the usual give-and-take that ensued over it, ate up the hours till her first set. Being cloistered with the musicians prevented any contact with other people, which suited Vichy. In her mind other people represented one person: Ben Larkin.

After making a wobbly start, Vichy settled down and the rest of the set went smoothly. During her breaks she hid out in her tiny dressing room, endeavoring to convince herself she was not nervously anticipating the last set.

After a day that seemed at least seventy-five hours long, the time for her last set did arrive, and with it the man who

70

had claimed the major part of her thoughts through every one of those hours.

Torn as she was by the conflicting urges to run to him and run for her life, Vichy somehow managed to render every one of her numbers without faltering.

Then the last song was finished, and, while aloud she said her thank yous and automatically rattled off her usual chatter to her audience, silently she shouted down the voice that suggested she take the coward's way and flee.

She had only three more days of her engagement to get through; then she could run to the safety of her home. Surely she could handle him, and her own traitorous emotions, for a few days, couldn't she? Of course she could!

Looking like a gift from the gods in gray trousers, navy blazer, and a muted shrimp-colored shirt, Ben stood waiting at the table she now thought of as his.

"You're very sexy tonight, both in voice and dress," he complimented softly when she came to a stop in front of him. "If the intention was to turn me on, it worked." Ben ignored her sharp indrawn breath and went on dryly. "But, first things first. I haven't eaten since early this morning and I'm famished. Run along and get rid of your makeup so we can get out of here."

Tell him now, the warning voice whispered from the deep recess of her mind. *Tell him you're too tired to go out. Tell him you're not feeling well. Tell him you're on the verge of a nervous breakdown. Tell him anything, but tell him now.*

Vichy knew very well that she should heed the advice of that tiny voice of alarm. *Then why,* she asked her reflected image in the makeup mirror, *did I so meekly obey him?* For obey him she had. At her slight hesitation, Ben had simply said "Go," and she had. *I was right earlier,* she decided as she wiped cold cream off her face. *It must be a case of latent idiocy.*

But, surely, if I play it cool, keep the emotional temperature low, it will be safe to share a meal with him? The blue eyes in the mirror stared back at her reproachfully. *But I want to see him.* She defied those eyes. *I can control the physical thing,* she assured herself before swinging away from the mirror.

Oh, sure, that tiny voice mocked persistently.

Ben was waiting for her, leaning indolently against the wall across from the dressing room. As she closed the small distance between them, Vichy felt her pulses leap at the slow, lazy-eyed glance he sent roaming over her body.

"I grow hungrier and hungrier," he murmured, reaching out to clasp her hand as he straightened to his full height. "But, for the moment, I'll have to satisfy myself with food."

Vichy could not even pretend she'd misunderstood his meaning, for just looking at him aroused her own sexual appetite. She was playing with fire, she knew it, yet, when he started to move, tugging on her hand, she followed him without protest.

As it had been the night before, his car was waiting for him. Unlike the night before, as if deliberately avoiding an intimate atmosphere, he took her to a brightly lit all-night diner. The food was plain, but very good, and Ben ate like he was indeed very hungry. Surprisingly, after her first forkful, Vichy found her own appetite whetted, and managed to eat almost as much as Ben.

After the table had been cleared and their coffee cups refilled, Ben slid a long flat box from his pocket.

"I have something for you," he said warmly, sliding it across the table to her. "A little Thanksgiving gift."

"But gifts are not given for Thanksgiving!" Vichy exclaimed softly, eyeing the box warily.

"That depends on what you're thankful for," he smiled enigmatically. "Open it. I assure you it won't bite you."

Handling the case gingerly, as if it might do just that, Vichy lifted the hinged lid, a small gasp parting her lips at the sight of the exquisitely wrought gold bracelet nestled inside. The word expensive was, figuratively, written all over it.

"But, Ben"—Vichy lifted shocked eyes to his—"I can't accept this. It must have cost an enormous amount of money." She started to push the case back toward him and his hand shot out to cover hers.

"Its cost is none of your business," he chided, his fingers snaking the shimmering adornment from its bed of satin. "Besides," he went on teasingly, clasping the bracelet around her slender wrist. "The dice were hot for me early this evening. This bauble is by way of a celebration of my run of luck."

Vichy's supper was suddenly a heavy weight in her stomach. How many times had she heard similar words from Brad? True, Ben's voice had not contained the note of feverish excitement Brad's had always held, but, then, Ben was older, more mature, than Brad had been.

Fighting the sickness of despair rising inside, Vichy's trembling fingers tried to undo the bracelet's clasp. Brad had always exacted payment for his winnings gifts. Payments that, at the time, she'd always been eager to meet. Did Ben expect the same type of payment?

Ben's covering hand stilled her fingers' fumbling action,

and as if he could monitor her anguished thoughts, he said, almost harshly, "The damned thing has no strings on it, Vichy."

"Ben, I—" The words dried on her lips as, glancing up, she caught the grim expression on his face. Was it possible she'd hurt his feelings? Had she offended him?

"I won't be able to meet you tomorrow night," Ben's smoothly controlled voice scattered her questioning thoughts.

"Why?" Vichy could have bitten her tongue. Her tone held a wealth of possessiveness she had no right to feel. Yet, the query seemed to please Ben, for the harsh angles of his face relaxed into a heart-melting, sweet smile.

"Because I promised Chad I'd be home for Thanksgiving," he explained. Leaning back against the plastic-covered booth seat, he nodded at the waitress when she stopped at the booth to ask if they'd like more coffee. "He has been staying with my brother, Mike, and his family," he went on when the waitress had completed the service. "He's content there, but he expects to see me when he wakes up tomorrow morning." He flicked a glance at the slim gold watch on his lightly haired wrist and grinned. "Or, I should say, *this* morning.

"Of course he does," Vichy murmured in understanding. Then, smiling wistfully, she asked, "Will there be the traditional groaning board at your brother's home?"

"Without doubt," Ben laughed softly. "Shelly, my sister-in-law, is a fantastic cook. I wouldn't be surprised to learn she's been preparing goodies all week, just for the one day. And she'll really outdo herself for Christmas. Actually," he went on seriously, "Shelly is pretty fantastic, period. Besides being a great cook, she's a wonderful mother and a meticulous housekeeper." A tiny smile twitched his firm lips. "She must know how to keep a husband happy, too, for my brother smiles a lot."

Hearing Ben extol his sister-in-law's virtues caused a strange twinge in Vichy's chest. What did it signify? she wondered in surprise. A touch of envy? Surely not jealousy? Thankfully, Ben saved her from having to identify her own emotions.

"You're going to miss being with your family for the holiday, aren't you?" he asked, obviously having picked up on the wistful note in her voice.

"Yes," Vichy replied honestly, then laughed sadly at herself. "It's silly really. I have spent very few of my holidays with them since I started performing professionally ten years ago." She shrugged, as if ridding herself of her sadness. "At least I'll be able to spend Christmas at home."

"You're not booked in the lounge through the holidays?" Ben rapped sharply, causing Vichy to blink in surprise.

"No," she shook her head, confused by Ben's intent expression. "I was hired as a fill-in for this week, and then again for the weekend after Christmas through New Year's Day."

"So that means you'll be going home—when?" Ben's eyebrows arched.

"I was planning to leave early Sunday morning," Vichy answered. "I want to be home by the time my folks get home from church."

"And where's home?" he probed quietly.

"Pennsylvania," she finally supplied after a long pause.

"Pennsylvania is a large state." Ben nudged at her obvious reluctance to reveal the exact location of her parents' home.

"Near Lancaster," she hedged.

"How near?" he insisted.

"Ben—" Vichy drew his name out in exasperation.

"Vichy—" Ben mocked softly.

Vichy smiled in spite of herself. "The price of a few dinners does not entitle you to a life history," she told him with prim severity.

"I haven't asked for your life history," Ben retorted sardonically. "Just your address."

"Fresno, California," Vichy lied promptly, blandly.

"You just said Pennsylvania," he sighed wearily.

"My parents live in Pennsylvania," Vichy explained blithely. "I'm visiting with them while I fulfill this engagement. I haven't been a resident of Pennsylvania for over eight years." That much was true; she hadn't been.

"Okay, what is your address in Fresno?" Ben asked doggedly.

Vichy hesitated, then shrugged, giving him her former address. It didn't matter anyway, she assured herself; she had not left a forwarding address with the superintendent or any of the other tenants at the apartment house.

Vichy watched as Ben entered the information into a small black leather address book, full, she felt sure, of a good number of female names and addresses. Every gambler she'd met—and there had been plenty in the few weeks she'd been with Brad—had all seemed to know scads of women, Brad included. It would appear, she thought bleakly, that gamblers liked variety in all the games they played. Vichy was unable to repress the shiver that shook her slim shoulders.

"Are you cold?" Ben asked at once.

"A little. It must be getting colder out; there's a draft creeping in under the windows." It wasn't a complete untruth. She *had* felt a draft from the windows.

"Then let's get out of here." He cast another glance at his watch. "I have to hit the road for home soon anyway."

They were almost back to the hotel before Ben broke the silence that had enveloped them since they'd left the diner.

"Are you going to be all right on your own tomorrow?" he asked concernedly.

After all the years of being alone, his solicitude was touching. The problem was, Vichy didn't want to feel touched—not by a gambler. Never, never by a gambler.

"Oh, I'll be lonely," Vichy admitted. "But, I assure you, I'll survive." Her short laugh held bitterness. "If nothing else, I am a survivor."

Ben shot her a sharp glance but, as they had reached the turn that led to the front of the hotel, he made no remark.

In less than five minutes after leaving the car, Vichy was standing before the door to her room, watching Ben turn the key in the lock, flicking on the light switch as the door swung in. He turned to her, and she felt her breathing become constricted.

Would he try a repeat performance of last night? Could she resist him if he did? Did she really want to? *Yes! No. I don't know.* He was standing very close and the nearness of him was clouding her reasoning facilities.

As he lowered his head she did make a weak protest: "Ben, no . . ."

"Just a little kiss to see me on my way," he murmured an instant before his mouth touched hers. His lips remained unhardened by passion, and within moments he lifted his head. "I'll miss seeing you tomorrow," he whispered, caressing her cheek with the fingertips of one hand. "And I'll be back Friday, okay?"

Vichy nodded, fighting against the sudden heat in her eyes.

"Will you miss me?" His lips had replaced his fingers and the question was murmured close to her ear.

"Yes," she gasped, telling herself she was *not* aching for him to kiss her again, properly this time.

"Vichy," he groaned, then suddenly stepped back, away from her. "I've got to go, I promised Chad, but—" He took a half step toward her before becoming still. His sherry eyes seemed to burn over her face. "You'll be here?"

"Yes, of course," Vichy's voice wobbled with the riot of emotions coursing through her.

His hand, strangely unsteady, came up to lift her face to his lowering one and he brushed his mouth roughly against hers.

"I'll see you Friday," he whispered. "Now, go inside before I change my mind and pull you into my arms."

He stood there, rigid with tension, until she'd closed and locked the door. Leaning back against the panel weakly, barely breathing, Vichy heard him curse softly before turning away.

Trembling with reaction, Vichy walked slowly, carefully to the bed. Sitting on the edge of the bed stiffly, hands clasped tightly on her lap, she stared sightlessly at the door, fighting the urge to jump up and run after him.

What was happening to her? she cried silently. What was he doing to her? She was not an impressionable teenager to be thrown off balance by the lightness of caresses.

78

Yet that was exactly how she felt, off balance, unsure, near tears.

Dragging her fixed stare from the door, she lowered her eyes to her painfully clasped hands and her vision blurred. Glinting wickedly in the glare from the overhead light, the gold bracelet on her wrist seemed to wink mockingly at her.

A "winnings" gift. A shudder shook her hunched frame, and a soft moan went whispering into the still room.

In her parents' third floor storeroom, at the very bottom of one of her cartons, was a locked leather jewelry box. Inside that box were some dozen pieces of very expensive jewelry: rings, necklaces, bracelets, earrings, all "winnings" gifts. Vichy had turned the tiny key in the equally tiny lock on that box six years ago. She had not opened it since then. She could have sold the pieces. She could have given them away, for they meant nothing to her any longer. She had done neither for a very deliberate reason. She had kept the jewelry as a reminder of how little real value such things possessed when given without true affection. Brad had never really loved her. His baubles had been offered as an inducement. And from the moment she'd backed out of that hotel room they'd held no meaning for her.

Now another man, another gambling man, had tossed his winnings at a salesclerk in exchange for a shiny bauble. The very night before he'd told her bluntly that he wanted her. Was his gift yet another inducement?

A sob tore at Vichy's throat and she flung herself face-down on the bed. What was it about her that attracted these men? What was it about them that attracted her?

79

For she was attracted to Ben Larkin, strongly attracted. It would be pointless to deny it, even to herself. She was worried—no, terrified—that what she felt went beyond mere physical attraction.

Rolling into a ball of misery, Vichy cried herself to sleep.

Thanksgiving was just another day to be gotten through.

After waking, stiff and uncomfortable from sleeping in her confining clothes, Vichy set her chin at a determined angle and told herself, scathingly, that she had to go on. That resolution firmly set in her mind, she showered and dressed for her performance.

Surprisingly, there were more patrons in the lounge than Vichy had imagined there would be on a family holiday. Grateful for their attention, she psyched herself up to giving them the best performance she was capable of. The enthusiastic response of the customers sustained her through the seemingly endless hours between the start of her first set and the final number of her last. And all through the day, with every slightest movement of her wrist, she was reminded of Ben.

In a bid to prolong facing her empty room, Vichy joined her back-up musicians at the bar for a nightcap, much to the surprise of all four of them. They had issued the drink invitation every night, and every night Vichy had politely declined.

Seconds after she'd slid onto a barstool next to the drummer, she was left in little doubt that they were aware, to a man, of her reason for accepting this night.

"It's a bummer, isn't it?" the lead guitarist grumbled

around the cigarette drooping from between his full lips. Obviously, he never expected anyone to reply, for he muttered on. "This working every holiday is the pits."

"Yeah," the drummer concurred. "My working on holidays is about the only thing my old lady and I argue about." He paused, then laughed, "Except money, of course."

"What happened to the high roller that was putting the rush on you, Vichy?" The lead guitarist inquired in a bored tone.

Vichy stiffened, but somehow managed to keep her tone light.

"He went home to spend the holiday with his family." As she answered she slid off the barstool. The one thing she didn't need now were questions about the "high roller." Shaking her head at the drummer's offer of another drink, Vichy proffered her thanks for the one she'd had, wished them all a good night, and made her way reluctantly to her room.

Tired but not sleepy, Vichy had a hot, tension-easing shower, then, after slipping into a mid-length nightie, and a belted, fuzzy blue robe, she curled up on the bed with the romance novel she'd bought in the hotel gift shop the previous Monday.

Vichy was at a very touching scene in the story when a light tap at her door startled her so badly she dropped the paperback onto the floor. The tap sounded again and Vichy's eyes flew to the face of her small travel alarm. Eyes widening at the lateness of the hour, she swung her glance back to the door fearfully. Who in the world. . . .

"Vichy?"

81

Although the voice was pitched very low, there was no mistaking it, and with a smothered gasp of joy, Vichy scrambled off the bed and went running to open the door.

"Ben!" She gasped his name as she swung open the door, and that was as far as she got, for Ben leaned forward and placed his cool lips against hers.

Without breaking the contact, he backed her into the room, kicking the door closed behind him. A bulky, crackly object he was holding in his arms prevented Vichy from getting close to him. When he lifted his head, she saw he was holding a supermarket-size brown paper bag.

"What in the world?" As she raised her eyes from the bag to his face, her voice deserted her. Ben's sherry-colored eyes caressed her face and a knee-weakening smile curved his hard mouth into tenderness.

"This?" he prompted, rattling the bag. At her nod, he murmured, "I had a feeling you'd skip supper tonight. Was I right?" Again she nodded in answer, and his smile deepened. "This"—he held the bag aloft—"my beautiful songbird, is your Thanksgiving supper, complete with wine."

"But the time. . . ." Vichy began laughingly.

"Means nothing," Ben inserted softly, "now that I'm here."

Vichy wanted to dispute his assertion, but in all honesty she could not. Nothing outside her small room held any meaning for her, now that he was here.

"But I have no table in here," Vichy laughed, indicating the lack of furniture with a wave of her hand.

Ben's eyes surveyed the room, then looked down at the beige carpet.

"So we'll have a Thanksgiving picnic," he decided, setting the bag on the floor and shrugging out of his overcoat.

Vichy's breath caught in her throat, as much from the look of him as from his suggestion. Always before, he'd been dressed rather formally in suits or a sport coat, complete with dress shirt and tie. Now he was wearing faded jeans that fit snugly around his slim hips and flat stomach and clung to his muscular thighs. An equally faded sweat shirt with a barely disernible college emblem on the front enhanced the width of his shoulders and the breadth of his muscled chest.

Tearing her gaze from him, Vichy squeaked, "A picnic? In here? How?"

"Do you have a clean bath towel?"

"Yes, but—"

"No buts," Ben overrode her protest. "Get the towel and leave the rest to me."

Vichy retrieved a large white towel from the bathroom and following Ben's ordered "Spread it out on the floor next to the bed," she smoothed it out carefully, frowning all the while.

Dropping to his knees at the edge of the towel, Ben placed the bag beside him and proceeded to pull foil-wrapped packs from it, somewhat like a magician pulling rabbits from a hat. As he placed each item on the towel, he disclosed its contents.

"Turkey breast sandwiches. Lettuce. Sliced tomatoes. Pickles. Olives. Potato chips. The plastic container contains cole slaw. Plastic forks. Plastic knives. Paper plates. Paper napkins. Two real wineglasses. And"—he paused for effect—"the pièce de résistance, a chilled bottle of Asti spumanti."

CHAPTER SIX

Vichy rested her back against the side of the bed and sighed with repletion. She had not even realized she was hungry, yet she had insisted Ben toss a coin to see who got the last half of the last turkey sandwich. She won the toss.

Vichy brought her glass to her lips and sipped her wine, gazing at Ben over the rim of the glass. He was stretched out on the floor across the towel from her, his fingers laced behind his head. From where she was sitting he looked long and slim and shatteringly attractive. Her gaze ran the length of him and back, coming to a crashing halt when her eyes met his.

"You have already eaten," he murmured teasingly.

"Wh—" Vichy had to clear her throat. "What do you mean?"

"That was a hungry look you cast over my person, songbird," he taunted. "Made me tingle—all over."

Incapable of coming up with a suitable retort, Vichy

lowered her eyes and took several deep swallows of the sparkling wine. Talk about tingling!

The atmosphere around them had undergone a none-too-subtle change. Up until now they had behaved like two carefree youngsters on an unexpected vacation.

Ben had teased and beguiled her by relating amusing, and highly colored she was sure, incidents and misadventures of his growing-up years.

"My mother always insisted she was afraid to take her eyes off me for even a moment whenever I actively participated in any sport," he'd laughed in remembrance. "If I was playing basketball, and she happened to glance away from me for a second, when her eyes returned to the court, they invariably found me on the floor, usually all entangled with another player, fighting for possession of the ball." He'd grinned ruefully. "She always claimed I suffered more bruises, sprains, and broken bones than any six other boys."

"Played hard, did you?" Vichy laughed.

"Well, let's say I put everything I had into it," he conceded. "I remember one baseball game in particular," he'd reminisced. "Mother was in the stands, of course. I was defending first base, and I mean, I was *defending* first base. The batter hit a grounder to the second baseman and came galloping down the base line toward me. The second baseman scooped up the ball and made a wild toss over my head. I jumped for the ball and came down directly in the path of that charging runner."

"What happened?" Vichy asked breathlessly, completely caught up in his narrative.

"He charged right into me. He flew to the right of the line. I flew to the left." He shook his head. "Hell knows

85

whatever happened to the ball! *I* wound up in the hospital with a fractured wrist and a mild concussion. Poor Mom. I'm sure I'm responsible for every gray hair on her head."

At that point Vichy had softened, for Ben had thrown back his head, laughing delightedly.

"Mom always said I'd get mine someday, and she was absolutely right. I have had Chad in the hospital emergency so many times we're all on a first-name basis."

"Sounds like the apple didn't fall far from the tree," Vichy had observed dryly, and then had become totally confused because he'd answered grimly, "I guess not." Then he'd immediately changed the subject, becoming light-hearted and amusing again

Vichy could not remember when she'd laughed so much at such ridiculous utterances, but it had been fun, and she'd enjoyed every minute of it.

Now, with one teasing thrust, Ben had created a charged awareness between them.

Gulping down the last of her wine, Vichy straightened up and began clearing away the debris from their impromptu picnic, all too aware of Ben's hooded eyes following her every move.

When the carpet between them was returned to normal, Ben caught her around the wrist and drew her down to the floor beside him.

"Ben, it's very late, I really think you should leave now." Suddenly nervous, Vichy tried to sit up. Ben simply rolled over and pinned her to the floor with his body. Startled, a little frightened, Vichy lay perfectly still, staring up at him.

"I've thought about you all day." Lowering his head, he

brushed his lips back and forth across hers roughly, then blazed a trail of quick kisses to her ear.

"While I watched the Thanksgiving Day parade on TV with Chad, I thought about you," he murmured, circling the outer edge of her ear with his tongue.

"While I ate Shelly's delicious dinner, I thought about you." He nipped at her lobe, sending a shiver down her back.

"While I watched the football game with Chad and Mike, I thought about you."

His voice was muffled against the side of her neck.

"And when I lay in bed, trying to sleep, I thought about you." His lips had found the wildly beating pulse in her throat, and his tongue was busy increasing its fluttering rate.

"You"—Vichy, her breath ragged, could barely articulate—"you were in bed for the night?"

"Oh, yes," Ben laughed softly. "Wanting to get an early start in the morning, I went to bed soon after I'd settled Chad for the night." His mouth climbed back up her neck to her ear. "It was a waste of time. I hadn't a hope in hell of sleeping. All I could think about was you and how much I wanted you there, beside me."

Fear, and all caution, gave way to the warmth invading Vichy's body. The scent of him muddled her thoughts, confusing her. The feel of his long body excited her past all reasoning. His murmuring voice touched a responding chord in her.

"I thought about you too."

His fingers twined in her hair and he turned her face to his.

"Hold me," he whispered. "Kiss me. Show me you missed me as much as I missed you."

Without pausing to think, Vichy curled her arms around his tautly held neck and touched her mouth to his.

"Vichy."

Her name was groaned into her mouth and her lips were crushed beneath his.

The feel of his fingers tugging at the loop in her belt sent a momentary flash of sanity through her mind, and she tore her mouth away from the seduction of his.

"Ben, no!"

"I'm a man, Vichy, not a boy." He whispered harshly. "I don't turn on and off on command." Pulling back to break his gripping hold, he gave a final tug on the belt, then, with trembling fingers, separated the edges of her robe.

His sherry eyes, glittering with dark red shards of fire, burned their way over her quivering body, entirely visible through her filmy nightie.

"You want me every bit as badly as I want you," he said raggedly, his eyes fastened on the thrusting tips of her breasts. Lowering his head slowly, he touched his lips to one hardened tip.

The flash of sanity was doused by a surge of sensual pleasure. His tongue, moving the sheer material over her aroused nipple, was exquisitely erotic, and, whimpering his name, Vichy arched her back to him.

She had surrendered, and he knew it. Sliding one muscle-tightened leg over hers, he moved his body slowly, while his hand made a caressing path from her waist to her thigh. As if savoring the feel of her, he very carefully slipped his hand under the hem of her nightie and ran his palm up over her hip and across her quivering abdomen.

The warmth of his hand on her naked skin set off an alarm in Vichy's head. Cringing away from him, she moved her head restlessly back and forth on the hard floor.

"Ben, stop, I—I'm frightened," she cried softly.

"Frightened?" Ben's head jerked upright. "Vichy, you're a mature woman. You've been married, and there had to be another man over—"

"No!" Her frantic denial cut across his confused tone. "There have been no others. I couldn't let anyone touch me." A shudder shook her body.

"Good God," Ben muttered. Then, dipping his head to nuzzle her neck, he whispered, "How long has it been?"

"Almost six years," she admitted reluctantly.

"There is nothing to be frightened of," he crooned into her ear. "I won't rush you. I won't hurt you." Lifting his head, he ordered gently, "Look at me, Vichy."

"Ben, I—"

"Look at me."

His hand was moving again under her gown, stroking, soothing, coaxing softness back into her stiffened body. With a soft sigh Vichy turned her head and looked into his shadowed eyes.

"You want me," he whispered. "I know you do. And God knows I want you. Don't think of the past. Let it go. Wrap your arms around me and cling. I'll take you to a place where there is no fear or pain, only pleasure, for both of us."

The warmth of his voice melted the chill permeating her

89

mind. His gentling hand reawakened the sleeping tiger of need inside.

"Kiss me, Ben," Vichy sobbed, giving in to that growing need. "Love me. Take me to that place."

Vichy's first thought on waking was that it had to be midmorning, as the sunlight pouring through the room's single window was strong and brilliant. Her second thought was, *Good grief, I'm naked as a jay bird!*

Fully awake now, she became aware of the weight of an arm laying at an angle across the upper part of her body, and, more important, a warm hand cupping her breast.

Ben.

Memories of the hours she'd spent in his arms rushed into her mind and, sighing contentedly, Vichy closed her eyes, reliving them.

He'd promised her a place without fear or pain, and gently, tenderly, murmuring softly words without clarity but with infinite meaning, with his hands and lips and his lean, hard body, he'd kept his promise.

Vichy had visited that place many times before, of course, during the six months of her marriage to Brad, yet with Ben it had all seemed so very different, exquisitely new, unexplored.

Perhaps, Vichy mused dreamily, that place, that realm of the purely sensuous, was like a kingdom with many provinces, each a part of the whole, yet different. A whimsical smile curved her lips, and perhaps—she drew her thread of thought out fancifully—each province had its own designated label—from ecstasy, through pretty good, all the way down to, why bother? A bubble of laughter was

90

tickling her throat when a stirring of movement beside her put an end to the fantasizing.

"Good morning."

Softly, his warm breath caressed the sensitive skin below her ear. Reacting instantly, Vichy moved closer to the lips that had released that breath.

"Good morning."

Turning her head a fraction, she touched those lips with her own.

"Did you rest well?" he asked, punctuating every word with a kiss on her mouth.

"Beautifully," Vichy gasped as his hand moved, palming renewed life into her breast. "Did you?"

"Beautifully," Ben mimicked, gasp and all, as her hand began a timid exploration through the hair on his chest.

His hand moved, seeking, creating new, exciting sensations. Turning to him, Vichy deliberately brushed the tips of her sensitized breasts over his chest, to be immediately crushed against the hard flat plain.

"Did I make you happy?" he growled into the hollow at the base of her throat.

"Very," Vichy confessed softly, sliding her fingers into his crisp, auburn hair.

"Shall I make you happy again?" he invited, sotto voce!

"Yes, please."

The warm jet spray of water from the showerhead cascaded over her body, clearing her sleep-fuzzy mind. She had wakened, again, only moments before, gasping in disbelief as her glance came to rest on her small travel alarm. The day was more than half gone, and if she didn't hurry, she wouldn't even have time for a cup of coffee before going to work.

Stepping out of the tub, she dried her body carefully before pulling the showercap off her head. With a single sharp shake of her head, she tossed the thick, dark mass of hair back off her face and, sitting on the closed toilet-seat cover, smoothed and contorted her way into sheer panty hose. Slipping into her robe, she pulled the belt tight, opened the door, and walked into the bedroom just as Ben was coming to life.

"Hi," he grinned, his sleep-cloudy eyes roaming over her slowly.

"Hi, yourself," she grinned back, returning his encompassing glance with one of her own. Ensconced in the disgracefully rumpled bed, his body naked from the waist up, he looked infinitely inviting. Reminding herself of the time, Vichy tore her eyes from the lure of him and went to the dressing table to begin applying her makeup. Out of the corner of her eye, she saw him stretch contentedly.

"All that physical activity builds an appetite," he teased around a huge yawn. "I'm famished. What about you?"

"Mmmm," Vichy murmured, carefully blending blusher into the foundation over her cheeks. "I'm dying for a cup of coffee."

Leaning back, Vichy picked up her hairbrush, a frown creasing the smooth skin between her brows as she contemplated her tangled mop of hair.

"Bring that brush over here and let me do that," Ben ordered, pushing himself into a sitting position.

"Ben, the time!" Vichy protested unconvincingly.

"It's not going to take any more time if I do it or if you do it," he decided firmly. "Now get over here."

Sighing her defeat, Vichy crossed to the bed, avoiding his devilishly bright eyes. Handing him the brush, she sat down on the edge of the bed, her back to him.

With slow, gentle strokes, Ben smoothed the strands he'd tangled with his thrusting fingers into a gleaming curtain that framed her face and lay docilely over her shoulders.

"I love your hair," Ben said softly. "It reminds me of sweet dark chocolate." Leaning forward, he buried his face in her hair, drawing the clean scent of it in deeply. Then, parting it, he planted a shiver-causing kiss on the nape of her neck.

"I love dark chocolate."

A sharp pain jabbed searingly through Vichy's chest and she had to bite her lip to keep from crying aloud. How many times had he murmured the word *love* over the preceding hours?

"I love the feel of your skin under my hands," he had murmured at one point.

"I love the shape of your mouth," he'd whispered, outlining her lips with the tip of his finger.

"I love making love to you," he'd groaned as his breathing slowly returned to normal.

But never once had he committed himself with the words, "*I love you.*"

Of course, it was much too soon. They had known each other less than a week. Vichy shivered as Ben bestowed another lingering kiss on her neck. The attraction between them was strong, very strong, but Vichy was long past the age of believing physical attraction indicated the presence of love.

Unsettled by her thoughts, Vichy moved away from the reason-clouding touch of his lips.

"What's the matter?"

Vichy didn't have to see his face to know he was frowning.

"Nothing."

She avoided her own eyes in the mirror. *Nothing, except that I'm very much afraid that I am in love, and I don't know quite how to handle it.*

"Why did you move away from me like that?" he demanded.

Vichy was not about to reveal her thoughts to him. She might be in love, but she was definitely not addle-pated.

"I want a cup of coffee, Ben," she answered with forced easiness, "and I'm running out of time." Pulling the slip-knot on her robe, she added, "Didn't you say something about being famished?"

It was not until the belt ends fell apart and the robe gaped open that Vichy remembered she had nothing on except sheer panty hose. *Oh, Lord,* she moaned silently, *why doesn't he go into the bathroom?* Hesitating with embarrassment, she slid him a quick, nudging glance.

"I thought you wanted a cup of coffee?" he nudged back, letting her know he was well aware of why she hesitated.

"Ben, please."

"Of course, if you've changed your mind." He ignored her plea, settling himself more comfortably. "Why don't you come back to bed for another half hour?" He held a corner of the covers away from the bed invitingly.

Impatience, frustration, and a flash of anger stiffened her spine. Not bothering to answer, she walked to the

94

clothesrack on the wall. Keeping her back squarely to him, she slid the robe off her shoulders and let it drop to the floor.

"Turn around, Vichy."

It was a soft command, but it was definitely a command.

"Ben!"

"Turn around."

If anything, his voice was even softer, but the tone of command was harder.

Lifting her head proudly, Vichy slowly turned to face him, unable to control the flush of color that heated her cheeks.

Ben was silent as his eyes did a survey of her body from head to toe and back again. It was not till his eyes came back to her face that he saw her own eyes were closed.

"Look at me, Vichy," he ordered impatiently.

Vichy felt her face grow even hotter as she lifted her lids.

"You are a beautiful woman," he said emphatically. "There is no reason for you to feel embarrassed. Especially with me." A teasing smile twitched his lips. "Okay, you may get dressed now, but I fully intend watching you. I find watching a woman dress is one of the biggest turn-ons there is."

"Ben, really!" Vichy exclaimed, made even more embarrassed by his taunting revelation. His delighted laughter sent her spinning around to grasp blindly at the clothes hanging on the rack.

Luckily she grabbed the right garment, and nervously conscious of Ben's eyes watching her every move, fumbled and tugged her way into the dark apricot, form-hugging sliplike sheath. To complete the outfit, she carefully slid a sheer silk caftanlike delicate apricot-shaded float over her head, then stepped into bronze-toned sling-back, slim-heeled sandals. Smoothing her hair nervously, she turned to again face Ben.

"Sensational." He approved her choice warmly. Then, to her horror, he threw back the covers and leaped from the bed, his amusement-filled eyes leaving her in little doubt he fully expected her to avert her gaze. Rebellion rose and, clenching her hands, she forced herself to run her eyes over him in an outwardly cool appraisal.

God, he was gorgeous! Not an ounce of excess weight marred his tall, muscular frame. Did he still participate in sports? she wondered fleetingly.

"Well?" he prompted, working hard at keeping a straight face.

"Sensational," she managed to drawl shyly.

Once again the delightful sound of his laughter filled the small room.

"You're precious, you know that?" he asked when he could again speak. Knowing she wouldn't reply, he warned, "Get out of here while you still can, songbird. I'll meet you in the coffee shop in fifteen minutes flat."

Amazingly, he was not only on time, he was two minutes ahead of his promised fifteen. Having finished her juice, Vichy was munching on a toasted English muffin and sipping at her second cup of coffee when he joined her at the table.

"Is that all you're having to eat?" He frowned at her meager breakfast.

"I never eat a big breakfast," Vichy replied imperturbably, drinking in his freshly showered and shaved appearance. He was dressed casually in dark brown slacks and a velour pullover in gold with a brown stripe running across the shoulders and down the sleeves. The stripe accented the width of his shoulders, and Vichy had to repress a shiver at the memory of how the muscles had rippled under his smooth skin. The palm of her hand tingled at the remembered feel of him.

Vichy felt her cheeks warming up again and was grateful that Ben was busy studying the menu and had missed her loving perusal of him.

Lifting her cup, Vichy, suddenly parched, took several deep swallows, for loving was the only way to describe the way she felt when she looked at him. *Oh, boy, you have really walked straight into it this time,* she told herself bleakly. At twenty-two one can be forgiven for acting the fool. But, to engage in the same foolish impetuosity at twenty-nine one was to be pitied.

No, Vichy mentally shook her head, *I can't be in love—can I? It's nothing more than a case of blatant physical attraction—isn't it?* In an effort to escape answering her own questions, she glanced casually around the interior of the coffee shop and had to bite her lip to keep from gasping aloud at the flash of unfamiliar emotion that ripped through her entire being.

Through a haze she heard Ben ordering his breakfast and she lifted her gaze to the waitress's face. The girl's expression mirrored what Vichy had seen on the faces of several young women seated in the room; the expressions revealed overt interest in an attractive male, and that interest was directed at Ben.

Although the burning emotion she was feeling was unfamiliar, it was by no means unrecognizable. With a sigh smothered inside her cup, Vichy admitted that what she was experiencing was common, garden-variety jealousy. She also admitted that, yes, she was undoubtedly in love.

Suddenly needing to be away from Ben for a while, Vichy, finishing her now-unwanted coffee, placed the cup in its saucer and pushed back her chair.

"Hey," Ben protested quietly. "Where are you going?"

"To work," Vichy answered, avoiding his eyes.

"But there's time yet." He shot a glance at his watch, frowning. "Why the sudden rush?"

"No rush," Vichy lied. "I'm having some difficulty with one of my numbers and I want to go over it with the guys."

Although his frown darkened, Ben accepted her hastily conjured explanation and rose to his feet. As she moved away from the table he caught her wrist.

"I'll see you later, okay?" he asked quietly, his gaze holding hers.

"Yes, of course," she began, then gasped, "oh, Ben!" as he deliberately bent his head to kiss her on the mouth in full view of everyone. With his soft laughter burning her ears, Vichy fled the coffee shop and the curiously amused glances of its patrons.

The remaining hours of that day and night and the following one seemed to run through Vichy's fingers like precious grains of gold. She had told Ben of her intention of leaving for her parents' home early Sunday morning and, although he didn't seem too happy with the idea, he did not try to dissuade her.

Ben, sitting at the same table, was at every one of her performances, complimenting her quietly each time she finished and joined him.

On both nights he insisted she go with him early in the evening for a light snack between sets. And on both nights he took her to one of the restaurants in the hotel for a late supper. And on both nights he ignored his larger, expensive room in favor of hers.

They didn't talk much, but they held hands and touched a lot. Late Saturday night, hours after they'd returned to her small room, Ben broached the subject they had been studiously avoiding.

"Stay with me for the entire day tomorrow," he urged in a deep, growling tone. "There's no reason you have to be home earlier, is there?" He didn't wait for a response, however, pressing on. "And I don't have to be back on the job until Monday morning."

"You have a job?" Vichy blinked in sudden attention and surprise, believing, since Brad, that *all* gamblers worked at nothing but the odds.

"Well, of course I have a job!" Now it was Ben who stared in surprise. "I . . . ah . . ." His eyes took on a gleam of amusement. "I deal within the realm of probability, so to speak. Did you think I existed on a private income or something?"

"No, well, er," Vichy stammered. "I don't know what I thought." She knew exactly what she'd thought; she just was not about to reveal assumptions to him now. And, anyway, he certainly had been unencumbered by employment all the past week.

"Uh-huh." He gave a slight shake of his head as if clearing it. "I assure you I do work." His tone scolded. "At any rate, I'll be involved in a new project starting Monday morning and that, combined with all the holiday plans Chad's made, which he filled me in on on Thanksgiving, my time's going to be pretty limited as far as getting away before Christmas." He paused to nip at her lobe. "Sunday will be our last day together until after Christmas. Stay with me."

"But, Ben, I told my family I'd be home by noon," Vichy explained. "Besides, I really would prefer not to drive home at night."

"All right, I can understand that," he conceded. "But you could stay until early afternoon. If you waited to leave until after we've had lunch together, you'd still be home before it got dark. It shouldn't take you more than three hours at the outside to drive to Lancaster."

As he had interspersed the request in between light kisses, dropped at random over her face and around her lips, Vichy, her senses going haywire, gave in. Early Sunday morning Ben made love to her so fiercely it bordered on violent. Murmuring huskily words she could barely hear, but really didn't have to, caressing her in a manner that brought her to the edge of exquisite pain, he defined, in action, the word ecstasy for her.

For all they tried to hold on to the hours Sunday morning, lunchtime came and passed, and the moment arrived when she could not put off her departure any longer. Ben carried her valises to the hotel entrance and relinquished them to an employee before turning to her to grasp her hands.

"You'll be here the day after Christmas?" His voice had a harsh, strained sound.

"Yes," Vichy whispered, feeling strained to the limit herself.

"So will I," he promised. Bending his head, he kissed her very gently on the lips, then, releasing her hands, he stepped back. "Merry Christmas, Vichy. I'll see you in four weeks."

"Yes," Vichy said again. Then throwing caution to the wind, she stepped to him, placed her parted lips against his muscle-knotted hard jaw, and whispered, "Merry Christmas to you and Chad, Ben," and, turning away quickly, hurried to her car.

It didn't strike her until she was an hour out of Atlantic City that she had completely forgotten to ask him what kind of job he had.

CHAPTER SEVEN

All the way home Vichy had to fight the desire to turn around and go back to Ben. But she knew she would not turn around. She also knew it would be pointless if she did, for Ben had told her he would be leaving himself as soon as he packed his things and paid his bill. Nonetheless, the urge persisted.

The day had started out crisp and clear, but by lunchtime wisps of smoky gray clouds had moved in to dot the expanse of blue sky. The farther west Vichy drove, the more overcast it became.

She was less than five miles from home when it started to rain. At that point she ceased berating herself for not giving in to Ben's plea that she stay with him for the entire day. She didn't particularly enjoy driving at night when she had any real distance to cover, and she particularly disliked driving in the rain.

Vichy allowed herself a long sigh of relief when she

turned into the private lane that led to her parents' home. As she had a few weeks previously, Bette came out to the car to greet her.

"Hi," she called, skipping down the porch's three steps. "You're just in time for supper. How did the engagement go?"

"Very well, actually," Vichy smiled. "Better than I expected."

Opening the hatchback, she removed her cases before adding, "The back-up group was first rate"—her smile spread into a grin—"it made me sound good."

"Baloney," Bette snorted, grasping one of the cases. "You always did sound good to me."

"Yes, but you're just a wee bit biased," Vichy laughed as they stepped under the protection of the covered porch.

"That does not preclude my being objective," Bette retorted, holding the door open for Vichy to enter first.

"Perish the thought that a college junior would be anything but objective," Vichy teased.

They were laughing companionably when their father came out of the kitchen.

"What is this?" he asked the room at large, "the giggle hour?" When the only reaction he received were two wide smiles, he grinned in return. "Hearing you two laughing together again sounds good," he admitted, taking Vichy into his arms. "Welcome home, honey." He greeted her warmly, when at last he released his tight hold. "How did it go?" He echoed Bette's question.

"A piece of cake," Vichy laughed with the realization she'd receive the same query from her mother. "I'll tell you all about it during supper." *Except for a few details,* she qualified mentally, *which I intend to hug to myself.*

As Vichy had expected, the first words out of her mother's mouth were, "Did everything go all right?"

As they consumed the usual Sunday night fare of homemade soup and sandwiches, Vichy outlined her week for them, then, as none of them had been to Atlantic City since the advent of the casino hotels, she culled forth as many details as she could remember about the hotels she'd seen.

Over coffee and her mother's out-of-this-world, wet-bottom shoe-fly pie, her mother shot a frowning glance at the window, now streaming with water from the rain that had become a downpour.

"I hope this rainstorm isn't the frontrunner of a cold spell," she observed worriedly. "I was keeping my fingers crossed for the mild weather to hold through next weekend."

"Why?" Vichy asked idly. "What's happening next weekend?"

"Josh and his family are coming down for the day next Sunday," her mother explained. "He's going to help Dad put up the outside Christmas lights."

"Won't that be fun?" Bette cried, her eyes fairly twinkling. "A whole day of rotten Robert."

"Now, Bette, stop it," her mother scolded, fighting a smile. "Your nephew is not rotten. He's just—well—more boy then most."

Her mother's description of her grandson sent a memory whispering through Vichy's mind.

She always claimed I suffered more bruises, sprains, and broken bones then any six other boys.

Had Ben, she wondered dreamily, been the same as rotten Robert at the age of five? Vichy had to repress a soft trill of laughter. It was darn near impossible to imagine the austere-faced Ben as a holy terror of a little boy. But, on the other hand, Vichy mused on, he had displayed a devilish facet of his character more then a few times since Thanksgiving night.

"Are you falling asleep at the switch, Vich?"

Bette's quip corraled her wandering attention and, blinking away the memories, Vichy smiled in apology.

"Sorry." Her glance encompassed the three others at the table. "I'm a little tired. As soon as I've helped with the cleaning up, I think I'll go up to bed."

"You don't have to help. I, being the absolute sweetheart that I am, will do the cleaning up," Bette offered magnanimously. "You can go up to bed now, if you like," she went on. "I will even lug one of your valises up for you."

"Oh, Bette, you are just too good to be true," Vichy praised straight-faced. "The only possible reward must be canonization."

"I've thought the same myself," her mother concurred, getting into the act. "Many, many times."

"Good Lord," Luke groaned. "Spare me a house of flighty females." He fixed a blue-eyed stare on first his wife and then Vichy. "Two of which are old enough to know better." Shaking his shock of white hair sadly, he headed for the living room, mumbling, "I guess the only escape around here is the Sunday paper."

Vichy, Johanna, and Bette exchanged glances, then collapsed into a fit of laughter, like three teenagers.

After she finished unpacking her suitcase, Vichy slid between the covers on her single canopied bed, and lay staring up at the frilly "roof," as she'd called it when she was a little girl, missing Ben more than she would have believed possible.

What was he doing now, this minute? she wondered longingly. And, belatedly, where exactly was he doing it? She had never gotten around to asking him where his home was. His casually mentioned "central New Jersey" had been less then concise. But, come to that, she had never corrected the erroneous information she'd given him either. As far as Ben knew, she made her home in California. He didn't even have her parents' phone number!

Talk about ships passing in the night! Vichy sighed aloud. It certainly didn't bode too well for any kind of lasting relationship.

Nevertheless, whether wisely or unwisely, Vichy harbored the hope of a lasting relationship in her heart.

The day after Christmas. The words, like a silent prayer, skipped in and out of Vichy's mind. Her last thought before falling asleep was that not since she was a little girl had she wished for Christmas to hurry up and come.

Vichy had been sure the days would pass with grinding slowness but, thanks to her mother, they did not.

With no place to go and nothing to do, Vichy dressed in jeans and a rather shapeless baseball jersey Monday morning. When she walked into the kitchen, she was glad she had. Her mother, dressed in slacks and an old flannel shirt of her father's, sleeves rolled to the elbow, was standing on a ladder, cleaning the paneling.

The kitchen looked like it had been struck by a mini-tornado. The windows looked naked without their curtains. The chairs had been pushed into one corner, and the clock and other decorations that had hung on the wall now littered the table. Stunned by the upheaval, Vichy asked the obvious.

"Mother, what are you doing?"

"Dancing," Johanna returned placidly.

Vichy grinned appreciatively. At sixty her mother's sense of humor was every bit as keen as it had been at thirty. Johanna's eyes twinkled as she returned Vichy's grin.

"There's juice in the fridge, raisin bread in the bread drawer, and coffee in the pot. Help yourself." With that she turned back to the wall.

After clearing and wiping a corner of the table and retrieving a chair, Vichy dropped two slices of raisin bread into the toaster and poured herself a small glass of juice. Standing at the refrigerator, she sipped the juice and frowned worriedly at her mother's back. "You shouldn't be up there," she advised.

"It's the only way I can reach the top," Johanna retorted dryly, then, turning to face her daughter, chided gently, "I'm not decrepit, you know."

"I know," Vichy shook her head in wonder. "You can work rings around most people half your age, but it makes me nervous to see you up there." She smiled coaxingly. "Why don't you come down and have a cup of coffee with me? Then, after I've eaten, I'll do the paneling."

Vichy and Johanna spent that entire week housecleaning. From the kitchen they proceeded to the dining room, and from there the rest of the house, up to and including the third floor. By Saturday morning Vichy's respect for her mother had grown to near awe. Seldom-used muscles Vichy hadn't even known she possessed complained achingly from abuse, while her mother, who had not only kept

107

pace with Vichy, but had blazed the way, bustled around getting breakfast as if she'd never heard the word *housecleaning*.

"You look like you've had a hectic week of debauchery," Bette, who had escaped the week's arduous labor by hiding out at school, teased when Vichy entered the kitchen. "Mom would make a great field marshal, wouldn't she?"

"A little hard work never hurt anyone," Johanna said blandly from the stove, where she was frying scrapple for breakfast. "*You* can set the table, young lady," she told Bette, then, "Vichy, go to the door and give your father a yell. He's out in the barn."

Feeling as though she should tiptoe over the tile floor so as not to mar its freshly waxed beauty, Vichy did as she was told, fully enjoying the sensation of time having slipped back to when she was a young girl.

Sunday dawned bright, clear, and mild. At mid-morning the quiet serenity of the house was shattered by the arrival of Josh, his wife Caroline, and rotten Robert.

As she clasped the five-year-old's body to her in a brief, welcoming hug, Vichy assured herself Robert was not rotten, simply more curious than most.

By late afternoon her own assurances had been sorely tested. Robert had managed to get into just about everything, keeping not only his mother but Vichy and Johanna running after him. Bette, having gone out with a friend after dinner, had once again escaped.

As soon as it was dark enough for the lights to be turned on, they all trooped outside to admire Luke and Josh's decorative handiwork. And, as if on cue, they all sighed

appreciatively at the magical quality the strings of stag-
gered red and white lightbulbs gave to the house.

"I can't believe there are less than three weeks left till
Christmas," Caroline groaned as they drifted back into
the house. "I have *so* much to do yet to get ready for it,
and I know the weeks are going to fly by too quickly."

For you maybe, Vichy replied silently. *But, for me, the
weeks will seem to drag by.* Suddenly afraid her yearning
to see Ben, be with him, would overwhelm her if she didn't
do something, Vichy hung her sweater in the living room
closet, then hurried into the kitchen to begin preparing
supper.

"Seeing the house lit up gave me an idea," Josh said
over his hot roast beef sandwich during supper. "After
we've finished eating, why don't we all drive to the Christmas Village in Bernville? Robert would love it."

Robert would not be the only one, Vichy thought in
amusement. Unlike many men, Josh did not suffer
through the frantic preparations for the holidays. He
loved every minute of it, and his enthusiasm was conta-
gious.

"That sounds like fun." Luke agreed at once, thereby
revealing from whence came Josh's love for the trappings
of the season. "I'll even let Vichy drive," he added teasingly.

"You're much too good to me," Vichy responded to his
teasing dryly. "But, you're right, it does sound like fun. It
must be at least fifteen years since I was up there."

"You're in for a pleasant surprise," Bette, having
arrived home just in time to sit down for supper, joined
in.

"I was up last year with a couple of the kids and it's

109

really been enlarged. The night we were there there were at least twenty tour buses parked in the lot."

Bette's assertion was proved when Vichy, Bette in the bucket seat beside her, her parents in the back, followed Josh's station wagon up to the crest of a small hill on the country road from where they got their first glimpse of the brightly lit tourist attraction.

It was not a real village, but a miniature one, with small houses and pathways all gaily decorated and illuminated, all of it on the private property of a farmer who began it as a hobby and wound up with an attraction that drew crowds of people every year.

Strolling the arrow-marked lanes, smiling at Robert's delight in the life-size cutouts of cartoon and Disney characters, Vichy suddenly ached to be walking, arm-in-arm—in exactly the same way Josh and Caroline were—with Ben, both of them smiling as Chad eagerly ran to view each new sight.

Which was pretty silly, she admitted ruefully, considering she'd never even seen as much as a picture of Ben's son. Nevertheless, the ache persisted the entire length of time required to see everything.

Vichy was ready for a hot cup of coffee when, cold and rosy-cheeked, they entered the building with a lunch counter. The room was crowded with tourists, and as she waited her turn at the counter, Vichy glanced at the clock on the wall in disbelief. They had been strolling around for nearly two hours! No wonder Robert had coaxed to be picked up and carried. And now she could appreciate Caroline's forethought in putting Robert's pajamas on him under his snowsuit. With approximately an hour's drive home, Robert would be ready to be tucked into bed if he fell asleep on the way home, which, from the look of his droopy-lidded eyes, he would.

After giving and receiving good-bye hugs and kisses in the parking lot, they went their separate ways. By the time Vichy pulled into her parents' driveway, she was wishing she had on her nightwear.

The hours of the second week were every bit as full as the first week had been. With the housecleaning out of the way, Johanna declared her intention of getting down to the serious business of baking Christmas cookies.

For the better part of that week Vichy and Johanna kept busy sifting, mixing, rolling, or dropping by spoonfuls. Luke contributed by shelling nuts, chopping candied fruits, and kibitzing.

The centerpiece of fall foliage and the delicate lace tablecloth were removed from the dining room table to be replaced by a worn but clean plain cotton cloth in preparation to receive the mounds of cookies as they came from the oven.

By Thursday, the square, solid table had been covered then cleared many times of its light burden of crisp cutout cookies, buttery melt-in-the-mouth sandtarts, chocolatey-rich Toll House, fruit-and nut-filled Michigan rocks, and many others in all shapes and sizes.

Vichy had not helped with the Christmas baking since the winter she was nineteen, and she loved every minute of it.

By the time Bette came home from the college she attended in Reading, every room in the house was redolent with the baking odors. The minute she walked into the house, Bette put into words what Vichy was feeling.

"Mmmmmmm, it smells Christmasy in here. Makes me

feel like a little girl again, all excited, and wishing for the days to fly by."

Of course, Vichy's Christmas wishing had nothing to do with visions of sugar plums, or elaborately wrapped packages. Her visions revolved around a tall, lean form, a pair of strong enfolding arms, and a well-shaped mouth that could drive all other visions from her mind.

Friday evening she sat at the kitchen table with her mother, boxes of Christmas cards between them. While her mother signed the cards, and Vichy addressed the envelopes, Johanna filled her in on what had been happening in their many friends' lives since Vichy had been home last.

That weekend the four of them, Johanna, Luke, Bette, and Vichy, decorated the inside of the house. Kitchen, dining room, and living room all received their share of a variety of ornaments from homemade to "store boughten" as her father described them. Every carton of decorations was emptied except the one containing the tree ornaments, as the tree would not be put up until the week before the big day.

The Monday of the third week, almost as if her mother somehow sensed Vichy's need to keep busy, Johanna announced over breakfast that she was ready to start her Christmas shopping.

Luke responded with a loud, exaggerated groan. Although he fully enjoyed decorating, baking, and even wrapping the gifts, Luke Sweigart hated the shopping necessary for all of them.

"Relax, dear," Johanna advised serenely. "You're off the hook this year. Vichy and I will do the shopping." She raised questioning brows at Vichy, who nodded her silent agreement. "All *you* have to do," she went on sweetly, "is provide the money."

"There's always a catch," her father grumbled, digging out his wallet.

The morning was bright and sunny, but there was a definite chill in the air that warned of approaching winter. As she walked to the car, Vichy drew a deep breath, and when she released it, a small vapor cloud formed in front of her.

"Where to, madam?" Vichy asked her mother after they were seated in the car.

"We'll start in Lancaster," Johanna answered blandly, giving no hint of the miles Vichy would cover before the end of that week.

Driving towards Lancaster and the large Park City Shopping Mall, Vichy's eyes caressed the countryside she'd grown up in. The fields, some dull brown, some with a dark yellow stubble from last summer's crop, lay resting and waiting for spring, and the expertise of the world-renowned Pennsylvania Dutch farmers to bring them to pulsing, green life.

Near the turnoff road to Lititz, Vichy carefully passed a box-shaped, black, horse-drawn buggy, the occupants of which were attired in the traditional dark Amish garb.

"They're still risking life and limb in those things, I see," Vichy observed, shaking her head.

"Yes," Johanna replied quietly. "It's their way. But I'm sorry to say that with the crazy way some people drive today, they are struck with increasing regularity."

Shifting a quick glance to the buggy's reflection on the rearview mirror, Vichy smiled sadly. *It's really a shame,* she mused, *for, probably more than anything, or anyone*

113

else, these people and their picturesque conveyances are the trademark of eastern Pennsylvania.

Vichy and Johanna began what turned out to be a shopping marathon in downtown Lancaster. By the time the week, and Vichy, had waned, they had combed the area. Collapsed into the overstuffed living room chair Friday evening, Vichy recounted their stops for Bette.

"After we'd plumbed the possibilities of Lancaster's shopping district, we buzzed over to Park City and spent the remainder of the day, and a fair amount of money, there," Vichy sighed. "Tuesday we drove to Reading," she went on, to Bette's amusement. "Not only did we hit just about every one of the city's now-famous outlet stores, but we also shopped at both the Berkshire Mall and the Fairgrounds Square Mall, on the outskirts of Reading, as well."

As, at this point, Bette was nearly convulsed with laughter, Vichy cut through the rest of her long list of places she and Johanna had stopped at, to end on a groan. "And do you believe we even drove all the way up to Allentown and the Lehigh Shopping Mall?"

"Of course I believe it," Bette laughed. "I went through the same leg-killing routine last year. But, 'fess up, it's fun shopping with Mom, isn't it?"

"Yes, it is," Vichy admitted, laughing with her. "I enjoyed every footsore minute of it. And, everywhere we went, the Christmas decorations were absolutely beautiful."

What Vichy did not admit were the number of times she caught herself thinking a particular article was perfectly suited to Ben. Should she, she'd wondered repeatedly, buy some small gift to give him on the day after Christmas?

114

In the end she gave in to the desire to give him something, and bought him a gold money clip, fashioned in a dollar sign.

Saturday evening Luke fastened a six-foot blue spruce into a metal tree stand, and within hours its aromatic scent had permeated the entire first floor of the house.

Directly after the Sunday dinner dishes were dispensed with, Luke, Bette, and Vichy, following Johanna's expert supervision, trimmed the tree.

Vichy remained downstairs for some time after her parents and Bette retired for the night.

With a glass of white wine and a record of Fred Waring's Pennsylvanians singing carols on the stereo for company, she sat curled up in one corner of the wing-back early American sofa, staring dreamily at the glittering tree. As had happened on her first night home from California, haunting voices from yesteryear came stealing into her mind, drawing her back in memory to previous Christmases.

"Mattie, if you don't hurry up, we're going down without you," an eight-year-old Josh yelled through the bathroom door as he fairly danced back and forth in the upstairs hallway early Christmas morning. Vichy, every bit as excited and eager to go downstairs as Josh, sat squirming on the top step of the living room stairway. It was out of the question that any one of them would venture downstairs alone on Christmas morning. They always waited for each other and went down together. At five, Vichy could have no idea that the thirteen-year-old Mattie was deliberately stalling in the bathroom to give their father time to plug in the tree lights and get the camera

115

ready to catch their expressions at their first glimpse of the pile of gifts under the tree.

"That's the most beautifulest tree ever." The awe-filled voice belonged to a four-year-old Bette. She had come to a dead stop at the foot of the stairs. Vichy, Josh, and Mattie lined up behind her in that order. It had been her first sight of the tree, because up until the time she no longer believed in Santa Claus, the tree was not put up till after Bette was sound asleep Christmas Eve.

"Oh, Tom, it's absolutely beautiful," an eighteen-year-old Mattie whispered in a tear-choked tone as she gazed misty-eyed at the diamond engagement ring her future husband had presented to her in front of the whole Sweigart clan on Christmas day.

Vichy blinked, and the tiny, shimmering lights came back into focus. Brushing impatiently at the moisture on her cheeks, she drank deeply from her stemmed glass. She had felt on the edge of tears all day, without knowing why, and now she told herself the tearful feeling was caused by the season and the realization of time slipping away.

Vichy had never been a regular-as-clockwork, every-twenty-eight-days female. And so it was that she, foolishly, had given scant notice when her cycle date passed early in the previous week. Her mother had kept her so busy she had hardly had the time to do any counting, but she should have.

The final days before Christmas were filled to overflowing with wrapping of gifts, and visiting friends and neighbors Vichy hadn't seen in over a year. The house rang with

116

laughter the day before Christmas with the unexpected arrival of not only Mattie, Tom, and Brenda, but a glowingly lovely Nan and her obviously proud husband Mitch.

When, soon after supper, with hugs and kisses and cries of "Merry Christmas," they departed for Williamsport, Vichy again had to blink against the onrush of tears.

Christmas morning was a quiet time. The gifts under the tree went unopened as, by mutual agreement, they waited the lunchtime appearance of Josh and his family.

The afternoon and evening was something else again. Once more laughter prevailed as Robert, being the center of everyone's attention, frolicked his way through the remainder of the day.

As swiftly as the day flew by, the hours could not pass fast enough for Vichy who, at least a hundred times during the day and evening, found herself thinking: *Tomorrow, I'll see Ben tomorrow.*

CHAPTER EIGHT

Ben.

His name was the first thing that popped into Vichy's mind on awakening the morning after Christmas.

Forcing down the desire to toss her clothes into her suitcases and jump into her car, Vichy joined her family at the breakfast table.

"Won't you change your mind about leaving today?" her mother asked from the stove, where she was stirring her father's favored oatmeal. "Uncle John and Aunt Katie are going to be very disappointed if we arrive without you."

"Not to mention Mark," Bette added slyly.

"By all means, let's not mention Mark," Vichy drawled teasingly. Bette laughed and, although she tried hard not to, Vichy laughed with her.

"Now, girls," Johanna scolded gently. "Don't be unkind. Mark is a very nice young man."

"But dull," Bette grinned.

Ignoring Bette, Johanna went on, "He's a conscientious, hard worker—"

"With both feet planted firmly in cement," Bette inserted, her grin widening.

Turning from the stove, Johanna leveled a quelling glance on Bette before plowing ahead. "Mark is kind and considerate. He's a good son, and will make a good husband and father."

"If dull," Bette, braving her mother's look, passed judgment. "And old dull Mark has been wacko over Vichy forever."

With a sigh Johanna turned back to her pot of oatmeal. Vichy hid behind her small glass of juice. Neither one of them dared challenge Bette's statement, simply because they both knew it was true. Mark Hartman had been "wacko" over Vichy, if not forever, almost as long as Vichy could remember. And, although every word of praise Johanna had uttered was true, Bette's judgment was also true; Mark was dull.

There was no blood relationship between the Sweigart and Hartman families. Luke Sweigart and John Hartman had grown up on neighboring farms and were lifelong friends. The titles of Uncle and Aunt were honorary ones, and worked both ways. To Mark Hartman, Vichy's parents were Aunt Johanna and Uncle Luke.

Mark, at thirty-five, was as set in his ways as a man twenty years his senior. Being the only Hartman offspring, he had been babied and cosseted by an overprotective mother every one of those thirty-five years.

Vichy had a sisterly affection for Mark, and it saddened her to admit that he could be summed up in one condescending condemnation: Mark never went out in the rain without his raincoat, umbrella, and rubbers. In a word—dull.

"I'm sorry, Mother—" Vichy began belatedly, only to be interrupted by her father, as he entered the kitchen through the back door.

"Sorry about what?" he asked, his glance shifting from Vichy to Johanna as he shrugged out of his plaid jacket.

"I've asked Vichy to reconsider her decision to leave for Atlantic City today," Johanna answered for Vichy. "I know John, Katie, and Mark are going to be very disappointed if we arrive there without her."

"There" being the large farm John owned in Bucks County, for which Johanna, Luke, and Bette were planning to depart directly after breakfast.

"I know they'll be disappointed," Luke agreed, but then, in defense of Vichy's decision, added, "but I can understand Vichy wanting to leave today. By going today, she won't feel rushed."

"Exactly," Vichy jumped in, relieved at having found an ally. "If I wait until tomorrow, I'll have only a few hours to settle in before I start working. If I go today, I can take my time, both driving down there and settling in," she explained patiently, for what seemed like the twentieth time. "I can have a good night's sleep and be fresh to start working tomorrow."

What Vichy did not say was that, short of a major family catastrophe, nothing was going to keep her from meeting Ben today as planned.

"May as well give up, Mom," Bette advised. "Poor old Mark will just have to grin and bear his disappointment."

She tossed Vichy a look of pure devilry before quipping, "That is if he knows how to grin."

"That is more than enough out of you, Bette Sweigart!" Johanna exclaimed. "I thought you liked Mark."

"I do!" Bette defended herself, choking against the laughter bubbling in her throat.

"She's baiting you, Johanna," Luke said quietly, pausing in the act of spooning oatmeal into his mouth. "If you're lucky, and you ignore her, maybe she'll go away."

"How can I possibly ignore someone who is mostly all mouth?" Johanna inquired sweetly.

"O-kay," Bette grinned unrepentently. "I'll shut up. I can take a hint."

The subject was changed and the rest of the meal was finished companionably. The name Hartman was not spoken again until Vichy mentioned it when her parents and Bette were ready to leave.

"Give Uncle John and Aunt Katie and Mark my love," she requested of her mother. "And tell them I promise I'll visit them early in the new year."

Finally, after assuring her mother for the third time that she would drive carefully, Vichy was alone. Turning from the door, she ran up the stairs and into her room to pack. Glancing at the small travel alarm by her bed, she calculated that if she could be ready to leave within the hour, she could be in Atlantic City by lunchtime.

Would Ben be there when she arrived? she wondered as she hurried back and forth between her closet and the open suitcases on her bed. What if he didn't show up at all? Vichy stopped dead halfway between her large double dresser and the bed. He would show up. He had to show up! Vichy bit her lip at the intensity of the anxiety that rushed over her.

She had not seen him in four weeks, yet just thinking about him made her tremble all over. Was it possible to fall so deeply in love in such a short time? Vichy was very much afraid that it was not only possible, but it was exactly what had happened to her. What scared her was knowing full well she had fallen head over heels in love very quickly once before. She had paid, painfully, for her impetuousness that time. Would she have to pay again?

Shaking herself out of her reverie, Vichy resumed her packing. Except for the fact that they both enjoyed gambling, there was no comparison between the two men. In complete opposition to Brad, Ben was mature, settled, and secure in the life he'd made for himself.

He'll be there, Vichy assured herself, beginning to hum snatches of a Christmas song she'd heard repeatedly over the previous week.

Vichy wasn't on the road too long before she decided that everyone and his brother were making Christmas visits. Although the traffic was heavy on the Pennsylvania Turnpike, it moved at a steady, even flow and she was making good time until she left the Turnpike and got onto the bypass around Philadelphia. The bypass was bumper-to-bumper with cars, and every one of those bumpers was attached to a machine with a horn. It seemed to Vichy that at least half of those horns were being leaned on by irate drivers.

By crawling, inching, and softly cursing, Vichy finally reached the Walt Whitman Bridge over the Delaware. After she'd crossed the bridge and driven onto the Atlantic City Expressway, the traffic was moving in an even flow again and Vichy was able to maintain the speed limit straight into Atlantic City.

After making her presence known to the management, Vichy went to the same small room she'd occupied four weeks previously and began unpacking, jumping in expectation at every sound of movement in the hallway.

Now what? Her unpacking finished, Vichy stood indecisively in the middle of the room. Had Ben arrived? Was he, at that moment, in his own room unpacking?

Just the thought that Ben could be that close set her pulses hammering and, unable to stay still another minute, Vichy smoothed the sides of her hair, which she'd coiled back into a neat chignon that morning, applied a fresh coat of shimmering gloss to her lips, then, scooping up her handbag, left the room.

The lobby was an absolute madhouse. Vichy could barely see the carpeting for the mass of humanity that filled the large area, After making her way to the desk, with repeated pleas of "excuse me, please" and "pardon me," she waited her turn with forced patience until the harried clerk glanced at her, a warm smile curving his lips in response to her own.

"May I help you?"

"Yes, thank you," Vichy hesitated, then rushed on. "Do you have a Mr. Bennett Larkin registered?"

"Larkin," he repeated, his eyes making a quick, expert perusal of the registration book. "No, ma'am, no Larkin. I'm sorry."

No Larkin. Vichy repeated the words dully to herself, shocked at the feeling of desolation that swept through her. Biting on the inside of her lower lip, she made a half turn away, then, on inspiration, turned back to the clerk.

123

"Could you tell me if you're holding a reservation for Mr. Larkin?"

"Just a moment." He stepped away from the counter for a few seconds, and when he returned, his answer was written on his sympathetic expression.

"I'm sorry, but I have no reservation under that name."

"I see." Forcing her lips into a semblance of a smile, Vichy murmured, "Thank you," and walked away from the desk aimlessly.

Ben was not here, and he was not coming. The phrase, circling around in Vichy's head, affected the nerves in her stomach. She felt sick, and suddenly very, very tired.

Moving without purpose through the crush of laughing people, she fought a silent battle against the overwhelming urge to weep like an abandoned child. It was not until she noticed the odd glances being sent her way that Vichy, straightening her spine, made a concentrated effort to pull herself together.

Coffee! Find someplace that you can get a cup of coffee, Vichy admonished herself sharply. *And don't you dare cry!*

Vichy made a beeline for the nearest restaurant. She ordered coffee then, as a tiny frown made an appearance above the haughty waiter's slightly hooked, long nose, added weakly that she'd have a chef's salad with the house dressing as well.

Ignoring the salad, she sipped at her coffee while trying to calm her rioting thoughts. Ben's last words to her had been, "I'll see you in four weeks." So, where was he? Had something happened to detain him? Or, and here she winced, hadn't he meant to keep his promise to join her today?

Vichy motioned the waiter to refill her cup and suffered the grimace he aimed at her untouched salad.

"The salad is not to your liking, ma'am?" he asked through lips that looked like they'd been sucking a lemon.

"The salad is fine, thank you," Vichy sighed, half tiredly, half exaggeratedly, picking up her fork. "Don't go away mad," she pleaded bitchily. "Just go away, please."

The affronted waiter withdrew stiffly, and, pushing the salad around with her fork, Vichy went back to thinking of the cause of her anguish—one Bennett Larkin. Dammit, where was he?

Possibly signing in at another hotel this very minute! Vichy brightened at this new thought. Of course! What an absolute nit she was being. She had seen for herself on her way in how crammed full the city was. The possibility was very real that Ben had been unable to secure a room in this hotel. But that did not preclude the possibility that he'd booked into another hotel.

Her reasoning had the effect of not only lightening her mood, but of sharpening her appetite as well. Suddenly hungry, Vichy dug into her salad. When she lifted her cup to drain the last of her coffee, the light became tangled in her gold bracelet, causing the metal to glitter as if it were winking at her. At least that was the whimsical thought that sprang into her mind with the reflecting gleam.

Hiding her smile behind the cup, Vichy told herself she had no more sense than a teenager, yet her optimism was restored to the point that she bestowed a brilliant smile on the now-confused waiter as she paid her check and left the restaurant.

Vichy stayed in her room all day, doggedly hanging on to her optimism as the day waned. At seven, her confidence slipping rapidly, she left her room long enough to have a quick meal. She was gone less than an hour, and after she returned she paced restlessly, berating herself for her lack of pride. It would have been obvious to everyone but a besotted fool that he simply was not going to show up, she told herself scathingly. And still she paced—waiting, waiting, waiting.

A few minutes after ten, tired, yet unable to sit still, Vichy paused by the desklike dresser to shake a cigarette out of the pack laying there. She had placed the cigarette between her lips and was raising her disposable lighter to it when her eyes came to rest on the already overflowing ashtray.

"Damn," she muttered aloud in self-disgust. She had cut down on her smoking drastically during the last few weeks, and now, here she was, laying down a veritable smoke screen.

Flinging the unlit cigarette onto the dresser, she turned and stamped into the bathroom. *You just don't learn, do you?* Vichy chided her reflection in the mirror above the sink as she scrubbed the acrid taste from her mouth with her toothbrush. *Men, in general, are not to be trusted,* she advised her bleak-eyed image, *and gamblers more so than most.*

She was wiping her lips with a hand towel when she heard the light tap on the door.

"Vichy?"

Ben! The hand towel dropped to the floor—and her own advice dropped from her consciousness—unnoticed as Vichy went running out of the bathroom as if the skirt of her robe were on fire.

She wasted several precious seconds fumbling with the

126

lock, and then she pulled the door open, exclaiming softly, "Where have you—" That was as far as she got before she was enveloped in a bone-cracking embrace.

"Oh, God, I thought I'd never get here," Ben groaned as his mouth honed in on hers. His lips were cold, but they warmed rapidly on contact with hers.

Vaguely, Vichy heard the door close before she gave herself to the sensations his hungry kiss was creating. Inside the protection of his crushing hold, she forgot the hours spent waiting.

"You taste like toothpaste," Ben grinned as he lifted his head to stare into her face. "You weren't going to bed without me, were you?"

Vichy felt her throat close with the emotion that welled up inside. Oh, God, he looked so, so—beautiful! She had known she was in love with him. But how very deeply in love became evident now. She had never been the clinging type, yet now, suddenly, she wanted to cling to this man for all she was worth. The strength of the emotion raging through her was frightening. Grasping at her swiftly dissolving sense of self-preservation, she loosened her hold and attempted to move away from him.

"What's wrong?" Ben demanded softly, his arms tightening to keep her close. His grin vanishing, he frowned down at her.

"Nothing's wrong," Vichy shook her head to emphasize her denial. "I—I thought you weren't coming," she rushed on in a whisper.

Ben's hand came up to capture her chin and give it a light shake before he dipped his head to kiss her mouth gently.

"I told you I'd be here, didn't I?" he growled softly.

"Yes, but—"

"But I got hung up in a family day at my parents'," he cut her off. "I had planned to take Chad there early this morning, stay a short time, and then leave to come here." He sighed. "Besides Mike and his family, the house was full of assorted aunts, uncles, cousins, nieces, and nephews. I hadn't seen some of them in years, and I just couldn't walk out on them." He smiled ruefully. "As it was, I spent the majority of the day glancing at the clock. I finally escaped after supper."

He paused long enough to steal a quick kiss. Then, releasing her, he ordered, "Get dressed and pack up. We're getting out of here."

"Dressed? Pack? Getting out!" Vichy repeated stupidly. "What do you mean? Getting out to where?"

Ben walked across the room to pull her suitcases from the top of the clothes rack. "I've booked a room in a motel on the outskirts of the city, practically on the beach." He tossed the cases on the bed and opened them before adding, "We'll be more comfortable there."

"But, I—" Her protest stuck in her throat when he whipped around to face her, his expression settling into harsh, austere lines.

"But what?" he clipped. "You *had* planned on us staying together, hadn't you?"

Had she? Vichy smoothed her hand over her tangled hair. She had really not consciously thought about what their sleeping arrangements would be, but, yes, she admitted to herself honestly, subconsciously, she had known they would stay together. Vichy felt her face grow warm as she whispered the admission. "Yes."

"All right then." Ben's locked tight expression relaxed.

"Surely you didn't think we could stay here?" A wave of his long hand indicated the confining area of the small room. "We'd be bumping into each other every other time we turned around. I stopped to check out the place and drop off my own stuff before coming here. It's large and roomy." A teasing smile pulled at his lips and his sherry eyes glittered at her. "And the bed's almost twice the size of this one." He jerked his thumb at the bed beside him. "Now, come on, Vichy. Pull a pair of slacks on over your nightgown, throw your things in these suitcases, and let's get out of here." He grinned rakishly. "I've got the car sitting where it shouldn't be, and I asked to have your car brought out."

"Pull a pair of slacks over my nightgown? Are you crazy?" she cried. "I can't go out like that."

"Sez who," Ben retorted. "You're going to wear a coat, so who'll know?" Now his grin was downright wicked. "Besides, it'll save time once we get to our room. If we even get there," he added pointedly.

It was the "our room" that did the trick. Vichy so liked the sound of it, she did exactly as he'd directed. The entire move, from packing to unpacking again, was completed in less than an hour.

As Ben promised, the room was large, an efficiency with a tiny kitchen area at one end and the rest a combination bedroom-living room.

"There's another reason why I was so late getting here," Ben said after he'd stashed their valises out of the way. Strolling into the kitchen area, he opened the cabinet above the sink and the door to the small boxlike refrigerator. "I stopped to do the grocery shopping," he grinned, indicating the full shelves. "Are you hungry?"

129

Suddenly she was, ravenously. "Starving," Vichy admitted, grinning back at him.

"And me," he agreed in a husky murmur that sent little tingles up Vichy's back. Walking to her slowly, he slid his arms around her waist and drew her close to his hard body. "But that will have to wait." Bending his head, he tasted her mouth with his tongue. "Mmm, yes," he whispered. "I'll have you for dessert."

All thoughts of food went flying out of Vichy's mind. In fact all thoughts of any kind dissolved, replaced by a burning need to appease the four-week-long hunger of a more earthy nature.

Sighing his name, Vichy curved her soft body to the rigid length of his, a fresh flare of excitement surging through her at his immediate and obvious response.

"God, I want you," Ben groaned huskily against her parted lips.

"I have wanted you continually for the last four weeks."

Very slowly, as if to savor every minute, his trembling fingers betraying the intensity of his arousal, Ben removed her robe and then her nightgown. Without touching her, his sherry-colored eyes sparking with red shades of light, he stood still, his gaze drinking in the sight of her like a man dying of thirst.

Motionless, her breathing painfully shallow, Vichy withstood his devouring glance until she began to tremble visibly.

"Ben, please," she pleaded in a throaty whimper. "I need you so badly, I hurt. If you don't touch me, love me soon—"

The room tilted as, with a half growl, half groan, Ben swept her up into his arms and carried her to the bed.

* * *

There is something extremely erotic about the glitter of gold when it is the only adornment on a woman's unclothed body.

Vichy came to life with the touch of cool metal against her exposed skin. The air was chilly and even before she opened her eyes she moved with unconscious sensuality toward the warmth of the body beside her. Her movement intensified the feeling of metal against her skin and, frowning in confusion, she opened her eyes and glanced down.

She had not been imagining the metallic coolness! Eyes widening, Vichy stared at the length of gold draped across the rounded fullness of her breasts. It was a necklace, the match to the bracelet that even now circled her wrist, unclasped and strung across her body.

Stiffening, Vichy stared at the expensive, glittering trinket that looked almost indecent lying there against her naked breasts.

What was this, some sort of payment for services rendered? The sickening thought jolted through her mind, freezing her already stiffened form.

"Merry Christmas."

The tenderness embodied in Ben's soft tone banished the degrading question. Twisting her head, Vichy stared up into eyes so warm the chill was banished from her body as well.

"I couldn't resist." A devilish smile pulling at his lips, his eyes shifted to the adornment, then back to hers. "It was wrapped so beautifully too." His smile grew to reveal even, white teeth. "Like a little kid, I couldn't wait for you to wake up and open it. I wanted to see it against your soft skin." Now his smile held pure wickedness.

"In my shifting around while opening it, the covers kinda slipped to your waist. And I just couldn't resist placing it on such an enticing spot." His face sobered and his tone took on the sound of an anxious little boy. "Does it please you?"

"Yes," Vichy whispered around a sudden tightness in her throat. "Very much. Thank you."

He was lying beside her, propped on his elbow, and now he lowered his head to bury his face in the side of her neck.

"I'm glad," he murmured huskily. "Because you please me in so many different ways."

Trailing tiny, exciting kisses, his lips explored her neck, her face, and then her mouth before he lifted his head again.

"You appear so calm, so self-contained, almost detached." Ben's eyes smiled, as if with a secret. "No one looking at you would believe that behind that cool exterior hides a very passionate woman."

Vichy's cheeks flared with warmth and she lowered her lashes at his teasing chuckle. She couldn't deny his assertion. How could she after last night? Her flush deepened as she relived in her mind the hours she'd spent in his arms.

After laying her gently on the bed, he had undressed with slow deliberation, his eyes compelling her to watch him. Once again Vichy had been struck by the beauty of his tall, slender, yet muscular form.

She had been burning for him by the time he came to her, and the fire consuming her had met its equal in the blaze inside him. Together their hungry fires had caused a sensual explosion. Touching, with hands and mouths and their entire bodies, they had driven each other to the very edge of pleasurable madness before, in silent agreement, they had joined together in a near frenetic search for shattering completion.

Now, her whole body warm with memory, a shiver feathered her skin as Ben's forefinger lightly outlined the ribbon of gold adorning her breasts.

"You're so very beautiful," he whispered against her parted lips. "And I'd love to spend the entire day right here with you, but"—he paused for effect, his warm, sherry eyes beginning to dance—"I'm positively weak from hunger for *real* food."

Feigning indignation, Vichy gathered her strength and pushed him out of the bed, onto the floor.

"Just for that, you get to cook breakfast," Ben growled in an attempt to conceal the laughter that erupted from his throat.

CHAPTER NINE

Thus began what was to become for Vichy a week out of time.

It was a slice of life's rarely offered perfection, beginning with the breakfast she served Ben that consisted of eggs, bacon, juice, toast, coffee, and his Christmas present, which he accepted with genuine surprise and delight.

After breakfast, bundled up against the cold late December wind, they walked the deserted beach arm in arm. The walk was to become a morning ritual for them, one that was always followed by another, more basic and warming ritual.

"I wish you didn't have to go to work," Ben sighed that first morning when they were once again cocooned within the warmth of the bedcovers and each other's arms.

"But I do have to go to work." She softly forestalled the request not to go that, she could discern from his expression, was hovering on his lips. "I have signed a contract."

Her eyes begged him to understand. "I have never broken a contract, Ben. Not for illness or any other reason. I can't now." She did not add that, as this particular contract was her last, it was a matter of pride for her to end her professional career with her record unblemished.

"Okay, I'm sorry." A rueful smile curved his lips. "And your assumption was correct. I was about to ask you to renege." He kissed her mouth lingeringly. "We'll just have to make the most of the time we do have together."

And make the most of it they did. They laughed a lot, and made love a lot, and, during the hours she was not working, behaved as if they were the only two people in the world.

In effect, what they were doing was playing house. Vichy knew it, but refused to examine it too closely.

Ben had made no commitment to her, nor had he asked for one from her. Yet, like a bud slowly unfurling to full bloom under the warmth of the sun, Vichy's love for him blossomed with each succeeding day.

They talked, at times casually, at others animatedly, about anything that came to mind, sometimes agreeing, other times arguing on a range of subjects, including politics and religion. And, although their conversation covered both the impersonal and the personal, not once did either of them venture into the future, beyond Vichy's present engagement.

If she allowed herself to think about it, it hurt, so she simply did not allow herself to think about it. Hanging on to each moment greedily, Vichy pushed all outside considerations to the very back of her mind. Included within those considerations was the beginning of a twinge of doubt concerning her irregular monthly cycle.

During her working hours at the hotel, Vichy's entire person, including her voice, reflected the happiness Ben so lovingly created inside her when they were closeted together in their so carefully guarded hideaway.

Ironically, now that she had made the decision to quit, her audiences responded to the new life in her voice with what amounted to wild enthusiasm. Being normal, Vichy lapped up their enthusiasm like so much cream. Also being normal, Ben displayed a delightful tendency to be jealous of every male member of her audience who evidenced the slightest interest in her.

Ben sat at the same table he had occupied weeks before, through every performance, glowering and scowling—to the growing amusement of her same back-up group of the weeks before.

By Tuesday, barely able to contain her own amusement any longer, Vichy, her lips twitching, advised him to go lose some of his money at the tables, adding, chidingly, "Then you'll really have reason to scowl."

Ben had the grace to grin sheepishly. "Have I really been scowling?"

"Enough to break up the group." Vichy nodded, her blue eyes bright with laughter. "Especially Ken, on the drums. I half expect him to fall off his perch momentarily."

If being the cause of her back-ups' hilarity bothered Ben at all, he hid it well. Lifting his hand, he caressed her smooth cheek with his fingertips. "Okay, sweetheart," he smiled tenderly. "I'll make myself scarce." He turned to walk away, then paused and glanced back, his sherry eyes glittering. "And, Vichy, you can tell Ken I said he should go take a flying leap."

After that Ben's attendance at her performances was spasmodic, but when he did show up, he made a point of buying her back-ups a drink after the set, bantering back and forth with them easily.

When the last set was finished Wednesday, Vichy had to go on the hunt for Ben. Up until then she had skirted around the casino in her comings and goings as if the floor had been implanted with land mines.

Her progress was slow, as the room was packed with people, all apparently eager to risk their hard-earned money in hopes of pulling off a fantastic coup.

Mentally shrugging in her bewilderment over the number of people who were avid gamblers, Vichy inched her way through the spacious room, her glance bouncing off the faces of strangers in her search for one dear and familiar.

As she passed one row of slot machines a telltale ringing and a woman's excited scream alerted Vichy to the fact that a machine had been "hit." Pausing, she glanced down the narrow aisle, amazed at the crowd that had gathered around the laughing winner. Silently advising the woman to grab the winnings and run, positive the advice would be ignored if tendered aloud, Vichy moved away from the excited chatter.

Vichy finally spied Ben at one of the craps tables, the sight of his tall form bringing a catch to her throat and increasing her pulse rate. He was standing rather indolently, leaning against the side of the table, and his expression bespoke boredom. Lord, he looked elegant. His fashionably cut, three-piece chocolate brown suit hugged his wide shoulders and slim body as though it were in love with him. His shirt was the color of thick, rich cream, and contrasted perfectly with his dark suit and hair. His tie was almost the exact same shade as his sherry brown eyes.

As if mesmerized, Vichy walked to him, her fingers itching to touch him, her arms aching to hold him, her body quivering in its need of his possession.

And to think I really believed myself in love with Brad, she marveled. Compared to what she was experiencing now, what she had felt for Brad took on the shadings of a teenage infatuation. What she felt for Ben was more than love, it was total devastation, and it frightened her. She could, with this man, lose all sense of self. And that was not good. There had been no mention of a future together and, with the way she felt, she was very much afraid she was going to be left completely shattered. And that was worse. Every ounce of common sense she possessed urged her to gather the pieces of her self that were left and run. But, as she had suspected of the woman at the slot machine, Vichy would not heed the advice either. She loved Ben as compulsively as any gambler loved pitting himself against the odds. She had to stay until the dice were tossed for the last time.

"Hi."

Ben's soft greeting drew her out of her introspection. Raising emotion-clouded eyes to his, she repeated him.

"Hi."

Suddenly his eyes took on the bright sheen of alertness, and she heard him inhale sharply. His attention to play was called from midway down the table, and with a quick motion of his hand he indicated he was out of it. Not once did his eyes leave her face.

"You want me, now, this minute, don't you?" he

138

breathed in a tone that reached her ears alone. Past all subterfuge, Vichy nodded.

"Yes."

"And I you," he admitted unsteadily. He drew a deep, calming breath, then moved abruptly. Scooping his chips off the table, he jammed them into his jacket pockets, saying tersely, "I'll cash these in later." Turning away from the table, he slid his arm around her waist and, bending his head, whispered close to her ear, "Let's go home."

Later, wakeful as she lay quietly curled against Ben's relaxed, sleeping body, Vichy decided that home, with Ben, was the most wonderful place in the world, no matter where its location.

Ben's lovemaking had completely immersed her in a hot pool of sensuality, washing away all lingering traces of shyness and inhibition until, in mutual hunger, she had taken possession of him as forcefully as he had taken possession of her.

His experience in the art far exceeded hers, as he had proved by his expert tutelage. That he had known, intimately, many female bodies before her own, Vichy had no doubt. That knowledge truly did not bother her. Ben was a mature man. It was the fear of how many women would follow her in the future that kept her wakeful. For, even at the most intense moments, when Ben's hoarse voice had whispered all kinds of exciting love words, not once had he uttered a word of commitment.

Did Ben feel anything for her beyond the pull of a very strong physical attraction? That was the question that was beginning to torment Vichy to the exclusion of all else. There were times she felt positive he returned her love in

139

equal measure. Yet he never said the words aloud and, until he did so, Vichy could not believe he loved her.

Don't be a greedy fool, she chided herself, blinking against the acidy sting in her eyes. *He has made no demands of you; you have no right to make any of him. Don't cry for the entire sky when you have your hands full of stars.*

By morning Vichy had her emotions under control. She would, she had vowed before falling into a fitful sleep, not ask for more than Ben was willing to give freely. That she had fallen in love with him was her problem, not his.

Her engagement at the hotel would be over with the last set Friday night, and though she had originally planned on leaving for home Saturday morning, she had subsequently agreed to stay at the motel with Ben through the weekend. All she could do, she decided now, was hold her love close to her heart and pray that by the time that weekend was over, Ben would have made clear his intentions regarding the future.

New Year's Eve was a gala time at the hotel, starting early and ending late—or rather early New Year's morning.

Although Vichy joined in the fun with the patrons that drifted in and out of the lounge, and she observed Ben doing likewise, they saved their real celebration until they returned to their room in the wee hours of the morning.

There, ensconced in the wide bed stark naked, they shared an expensive bottle of champagne and each other. If Vichy had cherished hope that Ben would make some personal declaration with the advent of the new year, she was sorely disappointed, for he did not. He drank to her health, to her beauty, and to her passion, but not a word about their future together passed his lips.

140

Friday Vichy woke disheveled and with a headache. Groaning in protest at the tiny hammers beating at her temples, she rolled over and forced her eyelids to half-mast. The sight that met her gaze was thoroughly disgusting.

Freshly showered and shaved, looking delicious in tight jeans and a bulky knit pullover sweater, obviously without any residual fallout from the champagne or the activity that had accompanied it, and grinning like a damned devil in the bargain, Ben stood by the bed, a glass containing a nauseating red concoction in his hand. When she fastened her bleary gaze on him, he held the glass out to her like an offering.

"What's that?" she groaned, fuzzy-tongued.

"My secret blend," he replied with twitching lips. "Drink it down; it'll clear the cobwebs out of your head."

Grimacing, she grunted "ugh," but she took the glass from him and sipped at the red liquid. Actually, it was not too bad, Vichy decided after the third small sip. Tomato juice, obviously, but what else? Tabasco? And? This morning her attention span was short, and, giving up the guessing game, she drank it down, as Ben had suggested.

"You're not much of a drinker, are you?" Ben observed in amusement. "You had only a few glasses of champagne. I can't imagine what you'd be like after an entire night on the town." One dark eyebrow shot up in question. "Or had you been drinking with the customers all evening?"

Vichy started to shake her head, and then stopped, gasping at the increased tempo of the hammering in her temples.

"No," she croaked. "I carried around a glass of iced tea all night." She paused to wet her parched lips with the tip of her tongue before adding, "I rarely drink anything other than a glass of wine with dinner."

"I'd say it's a good thing," he laughed. Sitting down on the side of the bed, he leaned to her and gently kissed her pale cheek.

"But I am relieved," he teased. "For a scary minute there, I was afraid it was the—ah—vigorous activity that had done you in."

"You're a wicked man, Bennett Larkin," Vichy accused reproachfully.

"Yeah, I know," Ben grinned complacently. "Isn't it fun?" Before she could retort, or even gasp at his outrageousness, Ben jumped to his feet. "I'll tell you what," he declared expansively. "Being the all-around terrific person that I am, I'll make the coffee while you have a reviving shower. What do you say to that?"

"Big whoop."

Ben's laughter followed her into the bathroom.

Surprisingly, the shower did revive her—at least partially. Then Ben insisted she eat something with her coffee, and the toast she opted for revived her even more.

By the time they left to go to the hotel, the hammers had stilled in her temples and, except for a gray dullness blanketing her mind, she was feeling almost human. Ben—the rat—was still highly amused by it all.

His amusement carried through her first and second sets. During the break after the second set he grinned at her once too often and Vichy, having walked the fine edge of impatience all day, slipped to the wrong side and ordered him to "get lost."

Not even looking offended, in fact looking more amused than ever, Ben drawled, "Whatever you say, sweetheart," and with a careless wave of his hand, sauntered toward the casino.

Tormenting herself with wondering if Ben's attitude was an indication of his tolerance of her, or his unconcern for her, Vichy watched him until he was swallowed up in the crowd, a strange foreboding settling over her like a shroud.

Ben did not put in an appearance for her final performances. And Vichy, torn between the desire to stretch out the seconds of her last professional engagement and the urge to have it over and done with, grew moody and depressed as the hours ticked inexorably away.

Finally it was the last set, and then the last song, and then she was thanking her audience with tears in her eyes.

It was over—the career she'd embarked on with youthful enthusiasm and high hopes had come to an end with a feeling of dullness and depression.

She had to find Ben. Now, more than at any time since she'd met him, she needed his confidence, his coolness, and, yes, even his teasing amusement. Perhaps, she mused, she needed the last more than anything else.

Declining Ken's offer of one last drink—for although the men in her back-up did not know this had been her final performance, they did know it was the end of this particular engagement—Vichy left the lounge and entered the casino.

As usual the room was crowded, and wondering irritably if half the population of the East Coast had suddenly had the urge to test their skill in this casino, Vichy picked her way at a snail's pace through the room.

The holiday spirit still prevailed, as was evidenced by the good humor of the majority of the people Vichy observed. At one point she was jostled by a young man at least eight years her junior, and her ego was given an unexpected lift when, after running his eyes the length of her and back, he said smoothly, "Sorry, gorgeous. No, on second thought, I'm not sorry at all. You're the best-looking thing I've clapped eyes on in weeks." Although his words were bold, his grin was shy, and Vichy couldn't help smiling at him. "I guess you wouldn't care to have a drink with me, would you?" he finished hopefully.

"No, thank you," Vichy refused gently. "I'm meeting a friend."

"Well, I can't be shot for trying." Smiling broadly, he winked and then moved on, in search, Vichy was sure, of more available game.

However, the brief exchange had lightened her mood, and with a small smile curving her lips, she would her way along the narrow expanse of floor space around the gaming tables.

She was beginning to despair of ever finding Ben when she was forced to come to a dead stop by a group of elderly ladies totally blocking the way at intersecting aisles.

"You girls should have gone with me to the cashier's cage," one blue-haired lady said excitedly to the others.

Resigned to being held up until they completed their conversation, Vichy unabashedly listened in.

"What's so thrilling about cashing in ten dollars' worth of chips?" a second gray-haired lady grumbled.

"It wasn't *my* chips I was referring to," Blue Hair snapped back smartly.

Controlling her smile valiantly, Vichy glanced around in assumed disinterest and waited for the mystery to unfold.

144

"Well, what or whose chips *were* you referring to?" this from a bespectacled, brown-haired lady.

"You see that young man at the cage window? The one with the lovely young woman hanging around his waist?" Ms. Blue Hair asked excitedly.

Five necks were craned around the corner of the intersection in the direction of the payoff cage.

Vichy was humorously aching to view a man with a woman hanging around his waist, lovely or otherwise. She knew she would be unable to see the cage window even if she did crane her neck, and she was too polite to shove any of the elderly ladies aside, so she stood still, waiting patiently for the explanation she knew was coming.

"Well, I never!" a fourth member of the party of five exclaimed. "Kissing in a public place!"

"Oh, that's nothing." Blue Hair waved her hand airily. "You should have seen them a few minutes ago, when I was at the next window. I swear, that young miss was all over him like a wall-to-wall rug. Laughing, and crying, and kissing him all over his handsome face."

Vichy choked back her laughter just in time to hear Madame Gray Hair query her friend.

"Why? Do you know?"

"Oh, yes, I know why." Blue Hair paused to make sure she had their full attention, which she did, Vichy's included. "I would imagine that young woman's display of affection has something to do with the thirty-four thousand dollars' worth of chips he's just cashed in."

"Thirty-four thousand dollars!" four awe-struck voices repeated aloud.

Thirty-four thousand dollars! Vichy repeated in awe-struck silence. The small dramatic moment over, the five ladies went on their merry way, and Vichy quick-stepped to the end of the narrow aisle, curious for a look at the winner and his solitary cheering section. The sight her eyes encountered froze her in place.

There was only one couple at the row of windows. The ash-blond young woman was very lovely and, with her arms clasped around the man's waist, she did give the impression of hanging on for all she was worth.

In between stuffing bills into his pockets, the smiling man allowed the woman to kiss his mouth. The man was indeed handsome. Vichy had never seen the young woman before. The man was Bennett Larkin.

Her body rigid as stone, eyes widening with an expression akin to horror, Vichy stood, barely breathing, watching the "happy couple." As the first tears rushed to blur her vision, another picture swirled around and formed to superimpose itself upon the scene before her.

Trapped forever in that mental image Vichy had tried so very hard to banish from her consciousness were a naked man and a naked woman, intertwined on top of Vichy's marriage bed.

The picture grew clearer, only now the naked man on the bed was Ben.

Much the same as she had done six years before, Vichy slowly backed away, her head moving as if in slow motion from side to side, the protesting words, no, no, no, coming in whispered tones through her taut lips.

"Hey, lady!"

Vichy had lost all awareness of the people around her and she jerked to a stop when she backed into a man. The face she swung around to the stranger was starkly white.

"Hey, lady," the man repeated in an altogether different

tone. The former had held hard impatience, the latter, sharp concern. "Are you sick?"

"What?" Vichy blinked her eyes and, thankfully, the vision was gone. "Oh, no, I'm all right."

"You don't look all right to me," the middle-aged man insisted, grasping her upper arms as if to keep her upright.

"I—I'm fine, really," Vichy choked. "It—it's so very hot in here, don't you think?" She improvised. "I'll just go and get some fresh air and I'll be fine."

"Well, if you're sure there's nothing I can do."

"No, thank you." Desperate to get away, she added, "I'll hurry out and get some air, if you'll let me go."

"Oh." He actually blushed, and at any other time Vichy could have appreciated the fact that her would-be rescuer was a very nice man. "Sure, but you take care now, you hear?"

"Yes, I will." Free of his hold, Vichy dashed away.

Huddled in the back seat of the taxi, Vichy had only a jumbled memory of her flight through the casino. She was wearing her coat, and clutching her handbag, so she knew she must have stopped long enough to pick them up before making a beeline for the hotel's front entrance. She clearly remembered getting into the cab and giving the driver the name of the motel.

Once inside the efficiency unit, tears washing her face, Vichy tore around like a demented wild thing, flinging her belongings into her suitcases. She was not thinking. She was reacting to a host of emotions; every one of those emotions screamed: run.

The door to the unit was open. The handle of one suitcase gripped in one hand, Vichy reached for the other case and went still, her eyes fastened on the glittering gold bracelet on her wrist. Releasing the handle, she unclasped the bracelet, and then its counterpart around her neck. Walking to the bed, she dropped the shiny pieces onto the smooth bedspread.

"You can go to hell, Ben Larkin," Vichy whispered bitterly. "And you can take your winnings trinkets with you."

Spinning on her heel, she crossed the room, scooped up her valises and walked out, closing the door quietly behind her.

Somehow she managed to get to her car, unlock it, and drive away from the motel, even though she could see very little through the tears that kept filling her eyes. After she was clear of the city, she pulled to the side of the highway and had a good cry.

Damn him, damn him, damn him. The words circled around and around in her head unceasingly.

How long she would have remained sitting there if a state patrolman had not stopped to ask if she needed help, Vichy had no idea. But, after she had assured him she was all right, she pulled herself together. She didn't have time to cry, she told herself bracingly. *Wait until you get home. Wait until tomorrow. But, for now, get your act together, and get out of here.*

CHAPTER TEN

Vichy spent what was left of the night and most of Saturday morning in a motel on the outskirts of Philadelphia. Up until she dropped, exhausted, onto the bed, she had, through sheer willpower, managed to keep a tight rein on her emotions. The reins went slack when her body hit the bed.

Fully clothed, her arms wrapped tightly around her midsection, she released the agony tearing at her insides through great, racking sobs that rent the silence in the room for hours.

Vichy woke around dawn, cold and cramped, wondering where she was. For a few blessed moments, blankness covered her mind. Then memory rushed back with all its attendant pain.

Groaning softly, she dragged her slender frame off the bed. Shivering, her movements stiff and not too coordinated, she stripped down to her panties and bra, then, ignoring the untidy heap of clothes on the floor, she crawled between the covers and escaped into a deep, dream-free sleep.

The slamming of the door to the room next to hers woke Vichy late in the morning. This time she was fully aware of exactly where she was, and exactly why. The image of her Ben laughing down at the young woman clinging to him like a leech was clear and concise in her mind.

Her Ben! Vichy blinked angrily against the resurgence of moisture in her eyes. *Stop it. At once.* Her Ben indeed! Her Ben, and that young woman's Ben, and probably a half-dozen other women's Ben as well. Damn all gamblers!

Suddenly she exploded into action. Flinging back the covers, she jumped out of the bed. She had to move. She had to get a shower and get dressed. She had to go home. She had to begin the process of eradicating him from her mind.

The fuel tank in her car was still half full when Vichy turned into the rutted driveway to her parents' farm. The power generator in her body hovered at empty. She had eaten nothing since lunchtime the day before. She was operating on nerves and guts, and it showed.

How badly it showed became evident to Vichy by her family's reaction to her appearance. Her mother fussed. Her father grumbled. Her sister, all mouth and no tact, was blunt.

"You look like you've been hit by a sixteen-wheeler. What the heck kind of week did you have in Atlantic City?"

"Hectic," Vichy understated dully. Had it really only been a week since she'd rushed out of this house, eager to fly back into her lover's arms? Her lover. Vichy shivered.

150

The metaphorical needle in her body bounced on E. The elasticity of her nerves had been drawn to full tautness, courage conceded the battle, and Vichy knew that if she did not lie down very soon, she would fall down.

"I've had very little sleep the last few days," she offered by way of an explanation. "If you don't mind, I'll skip supper and go right to bed. I'll tell you all about it tomorrow."

Tomorrow. The word haunted Vichy in the days that followed. So many tomorrows, and every one of them empty, meaningless. And the hardest thing for her to bear was the realization that throughout every morning, noon, and night of every one of those tomorrows she would continue to love Bennett Larkin. She wanted to hate him. She tried desperately to hate him. With ruthless determination, she recreated the setting in which she had last seen him. She remembered everything in minute detail, down to the shimmering gleam in Ben's eyes, and the tiny mole on the ash-blonde's temple. It hurt to review the scene, but it changed nothing. She loved him.

Thankfully, her parents accepted her hastily formed explanation of a week filled with work as she knocked herself out entertaining wildly celebrating crowds of people. But Vichy was not too sure of Bette. Bette was definitely casting her some very pained glances.

Two weeks after her flight from Atlantic City Bette's glances were the least of Vichy's problems.

It was on this Saturday morning in mid-January that the seed of doubt Vichy had buried in the farthest reaches of her consciousness reached full germination and poked its questioning sprout into the forefront of her mind.

Telling herself her suspicions were ridiculous, she

nonetheless took out her personal calendar and flipped through the pages until she came to the last one with a date circled in red. One careful count forward from that circled date was all the confirmation she required.

She was pregnant!

Feeling like she had received a stunning blow to her solar plexis, Vichy sank limply onto the edge of her bed. *Fool, fool, fool,* she berated herself mercilessly. But she *had* been told she would probably never be able to have a child and, even though that had been almost six years ago, she had had no reason to suspect that conditions had changed.

Had Ben assumed she was on the pill? He must have, Vichy decided wearily. For not once had he raised the subject.

What am I going to do? she cried silently. *You're going to have a baby,* the answer came from within. *Ben's baby.*

Ben's baby.

A small flicker of anticipation tickled her stomach. She had very little money, and though she had had several job interviews this last week, she had no definite prospects of employment. Yet, suddenly, she didn't care. She was going to have Ben's baby!

Sunday the Hartman family came to visit. John and Katie had changed very little since the last time Vichy had seen them. Mark had not changed at all; he was gentle, he was kind, he was considerate—he was dull as old dishwater.

Distracted by thoughts of her condition, and how to go about handling it, Vichy was totally unaware of the soulful glances Mark shyly cast at her.

Bette, however, had witnessed every one of Mark's

longing looks. After the Hartmans' departure, she launched a teasing attack on Vichy.

"If worse comes to worst," she grinned impishly, "you can always marry old Mark."

"What do you mean if worse comes to worst?" Startled, Vichy stared at Bette. Had her sister, somehow, guessed her condition?

"I mean, if you have no luck finding a job," Bette laughed. "Poor old Mark is positively besotted with you."

"Don't be ridiculous," Vichy retorted, weak with relief.

"I'm not!" Bette protested. "He's always been crazy about you and, unbelieveably, he has not changed a bit in all these years. When we visited them the day after Christmas, he bent my ear all day with questions about you."

"I like Mark, I really do," Vichy offered seriously. "But . . ."

"Yeah." Bette filled in where Vichy trailed off. "I know what you mean."

Early Monday morning Vichy drove to a clinic in Lancaster to have a pregnancy test to satisfy any lingering doubt. The results were positive. Strangely, it was not until after Vichy was faced with the reality of her condition that she experienced her first bout of morning sickness.

Saturday morning she was in the bathroom, hanging over the bowl, when Bette came tearing into the room without knocking.

"Vichy, do you—" She broke off what she was going to ask to exclaim, "Hey, are you sick?"

Waving with a backward swing of her hand, Vichy, appalled at being caught, gasped, "Bette, please, go away.

It's just a stomach upset." She barely got the last word out when a racking heave shuddered through her body.

"That's more than a stomach upset," Bette declared worriedly. "You have probably got some kind of virus. I'm going to tell Mom to call the doctor."

"No!" Vichy ordered sharply. "Don't bother Mom, I don't need a doctor." But again her body betrayed her with its violent roiling.

"We'll let Mom decide," Bette said, turning to the door.

"Bette, wait, please!"

"But you're sick, I—"

"I'm pregnant." Defeat coated Vichy's whispery voice.

"You're—" Bette cried in disbelief. "Does Mom know?"

The spasms over, Vichy shook her head as she straightened. "No. I just got confirmation myself a few days ago." Vichy sighed wearily. "Look, wait for me in my bedroom while I wash my face and brush my teeth. We'll talk then."

Bette was waiting, a frown creasing her smooth young brow. "This is incredible," she said softly when Vichy had closed the door. "How did this happen?" With a wave of her hand and a grimace she canceled the question. "Well, I know how it happened. What I mean is, when? Who? Were you seeing some man in California? Is that why you came home?"

"No, no," Vichy answered, sinking onto the bed. "It happened when I played Atlantic City in November. I—I met this man . . ."

"You hopped into bed with a stranger!"

Vichy winced at her sister's shocked expression.

"Please, Bette, keep your voice down," she urged. "And, no, I didn't just hop into bed with a stranger." Yet,

154

wasn't that exactly what she had done? she accused herself. The thought hurt, and she rushed on, "He—I—oh, Bette, what difference does it make?"

"Well, what does he say about it?" Bette asked bluntly.

"He doesn't know," Vichy murmured. "And he's not going to know," she added much more firmly.

"Not going to know?" Bette repeated in confusion. "But, why? He's the father. He has every right, not to mention responsibility, to know."

A tormenting vision, never far from the front of her consciousness, of a lovely young woman kissing Ben's smiling lips swam before Vichy's eyes.

"He has *no* rights," she said harshly. "And I'll take the responsibility."

"You're not thinking of doing this alone?" Bette demanded in a tone of shock.

"Why not?" Vichy countered. "A lot of women are today. It's the 'in' thing." If her own voice lacked conviction, Bette's did not.

"Not around here, it isn't. Oh, it happens, sure, but it is not the in thing. And certainly *not* in this family," she underlined darkly.

There was the crux of Vichy's concern. In a sense, she had been the pioneer of the family. She had been the first ever to enter the field of entertainment. The first ever to divorce a mate. Now Bette had just confirmed her own fears. Her latest *first* was going to go over like a lead balloon. Biting her lip, she eyed her sister wearily.

"I'm going to do it, Bette," she sighed. "They'll just have to get used to it. I know they'll all be shocked, but . . ." Her voice whispered away.

"I don't think shocked quite covers it," Bette warned.

155

"I can imagine Josh's reaction, and *Mattie!*" Bette shuddered. "I used to envy you," she confessed. "I don't anymore." She lifted her shoulders helplessly. "When are you going to tell the folks?"

"Soon."

Nodding, Bette walked to the door. "I—I wish there was something I could do," she said softly, not looking back.

"There isn't," Vichy swallowed against the lump in her throat. "But, thanks, anyway."

After that, Vichy knew she would have to talk to her parents very soon or take the risk of betraying herself to her mother in the same way she had to Bette. Yet, the day slipped by, and still she hesitated.

While her parents were in church on Sunday, Vichy, cooking the midday meal, decided she'd speak to them as soon as dinner was over.

Growing more tense by the minute, Vichy greeted the appearance of Mark Hartman at the door, like a stay-of-execution, while she and Bette were finishing up the dishes.

After exchanging small talk with her parents, Mark, ever the same, challenged Vichy to a game of checkers, exactly as he had when they had both been teenagers. Sighing in a combination of amusement and frustration, Vichy accepted his shyly worded challenge, exactly as she always had.

They were into their fourth game when the doorbell rang. As she was losing for the fourth time, Vichy, glad for any distraction, sprang to her feet.

"I'll get it," she cried, forestalling her father, who had begun folding the paper he was reading.

Vichy walked out of the room into the vestibule and opened the door. She froze, her hand gripping the knob.

"Hello, Vichy."

Ben looked leaner than ever, and meaner then a midwinter blizzard out of the northwest.

"If you slam that door, I'll kick it in," he warned softly, correctly reading her intentions.

Vichy moistened her lips. "What do you want?" she croaked.

A cynical smile twisted his lips and Vichy shivered. He looked tired and exasperated and mad enough to chew nails—very large ones.

"I want an explanation," Ben gritted out. "In fact, I want several."

"I can't t-talk now," Vichy, actually frightened, stuttered. "We—we have a g-guest, and—"

"Vichy, invite whoever it is in, and close the door," her father called impatiently. "I'm not paying to heat the front porch."

Rebellion flared. She couldn't bear to be in the same room with him. It hurt her just to look at him. How could she possibly go through the motions of introducing him to her family as a casual acquaintance? She was pregnant with his child, for heaven's sake! She just could not. Her arm moved to close the door on his face.

"You heard the man." A small, unpleasant smile tugging at the straight line that slashed his face, Ben stepped forward, forcing her to back up to avoid physical contact.

"Do you know what you're doing?" she muttered as he passed her.

"Yes," Ben hissed. "Do you?" There was no time to try

157

even to formulate an answer, for Bette came clattering down the stairs, a questioning grin on her face.

"Hi, I'm Bette . . ." She paused expectantly, her grin widening.

In an instant, Ben's entire mien changed. Returning her grin, he offered his hand. "Hi, Ben Larkin."

"Well, Ben Larkin, why don't you take your coat off and come inside?" Bette invited.

Up until that moment Vichy hadn't even noticed that he was wearing a coat. But, of course he was wearing a coat, she chided herself as she held out her icy cold hand for the garment. It's January.

Clamping down firmly on a rising feeling of hysteria, Vichy led the way into the living room and managed to get through the ensuing introductions coherently.

With every one of her senses alive to the smallest nuance about him, Vichy felt rather then saw him tense when she introduced Mark. Yet, nothing about his demeanor betrayed that tension.

He was all charm as he accepted her mother's offer of a cup of hot coffee, and smiled with devastating effect when Bette eagerly requested the honor of performing the small task of bringing it to him.

Before he was in the room five minutes he had not only Bette but her parents as well hanging on his every word.

As to the contents of his words, Vichy hadn't a clue, until she heard, and registered, the word *California*. Gathering her emotion-rattled thoughts, she forced herself to attention.

"The plane landed in Philly a few hours ago," Ben was saying. "I thought since I was this close, I'd drop in and see Vich."

158

His use of her shortened nickname was a dead give-away. He might appear easy and relaxed to every other person in the room, but Vichy knew better. The only times Ben had ever called her Vich was when he was annoyed or angry with her. Vichy had the sinking sensation that he was very, very angry with her. Once again she dragged her attention to what he was saying.

"No, we didn't meet in California," Ben answered a question posed by her mother. "Actually, I met Vich while she was performing in Atlantic City Thanksgiving week."

Attuned only to Ben, Vichy completely missed Bette's suddenly electrified appearance.

What was her father asking now? Something about whether Ben had much more driving to do today.

"The weather service is predicting snow for early this evening, you know," Luke cautioned.

"Yes, sir, I did know," Ben replied respectfully. "I'm not going to be driving anymore today." He smiled. "At least, no more than to get to the room I booked for the night." He mentioned a motel on the highway less than ten miles from Vichy's parents' farmhouse.

Vichy's spirits hit rock bottom. She had been harboring a hope that he'd be starting for home when he departed. Now that hope was shattered, and she knew there was no way she could avoid the coming confrontation between them.

Mark, sitting across from her on the other side of the table that still held their unfinished checkers game, stirred restlessly, catching her eye. Unbelievably, until he moved, Vichy had forgotten he was there.

"I guess I'd better be going," he said in his halting, shy

way in answer to her questioning glance. "I hate driving in the snow."

Ignoring the sardonic expression that passed fleetingly over Ben's face, Vichy rose to see Mark to the door.

As he put on his jacket in the comparative privacy of the vestibule, Mark proved that though he was dull, he was in no way dense.

"He's important to you, isn't he?" Mark asked softly, giving evidence that while her family had centered all their attention on Ben, he had been observing her.

Loath to lie to him, Vichy nodded reluctantly.

"I thought so," Mark stared at her, his dying hope reflected in his eyes. "Is there anything I can do?"

Strangely, dull old Mark was apparently the only one who had sensed trouble between Vichy and Ben. Grateful for his offer, Vichy nonetheless shook her head.

"You're a good friend, Mark," she murmured. "But . . ." Again she shook her head.

"Well," Mark fiddled with the doorknob. "If you need a friend anytime, call me."

Even though she knew she never would, Vichy promised, "I will. Thank you, Mark."

When she stepped through the archway into the living room, she found Ben on his feet.

"No, thanks anyway. I had a late lunch," he was saying to her mother, who had, apparently, invited him to supper. "I have to be going too." Striding across the room, he put a staying hand on Vichy's arm as she turned to show him out. "I can find the door by myself," he clipped. "I'll call you," he added in a tone that warned: You'd better answer.

Vichy fielded her parents' questions about Ben through

supper. At least she didn't have to parry Bette's blunt queries, as her sister had gone to visit a girl friend. She was beginning to grow desperate for innocuous answers when the phone rang.

Tossing down her dishtowel, she volunteered, "I'll get it," as she headed for the vestibule and the small table on which the phone rested.

"Get over here," Ben ordered an instant after she'd said hello. "And I mean *now.*"

Why had she assumed he'd wait until tomorrow to call? she wondered wildly. Did he ever do anything she assumed he would? He didn't even give her time to refuse. Harshly repeating, "Now, Vich," he slammed down his receiver after growling a room number.

I won't go, Vichy thought defiantly. *He can't order me around like a recalcitrant child. I will not go. What can he do about it, anyway? Come back here and raise all kinds of hell,* the answer came loud and clear to her mind. Releasing the death grip she still had on the receiver, Vichy walked to the vestibule closet for her coat.

Vichy's headlights cut through the darkness of the cloud-shrouded early evening, and in her preoccupation, Vichy was unaware of passing her father's car, Bette behind the wheel, moving in the opposite direction.

There were only four cars parked in the motel lot. Her palms damp inside her driving gloves, Vichy maneuvered the Pinto into the lined slot beside Ben's familiar Grand Prix. He must have been watching for her, for the door of his room was pulled open as she hesitantly lifted her hand to knock on it.

Her feet responding to her shaky order to move, Vichy walked into the brightly lit room.

CHAPTER ELEVEN

"Are you pregnant?"

The harshly worded question hit her with all the force of a hurtled missile. The slam of the door was an indication of the fury riding the man who had flung the verbal stone.

Struck speechless by the swiftness of his attack, Vichy stood motionless, her spine rigid with apprehension and the beginnings of a fury of her own. Bette! It had to have been Bette. When she didn't respond, he moved to stand in front of her, hands on his slim, jean-clad hips, his eyes blazing with red sparks, his expression grim.

"Answer me, damn you," he ordered between teeth clenched in rage.

"Yes." Vichy spat the admission at him. "Yes, I'm pregnant . . . so what?" Her question held a degree of bravado she was far from feeling.

"So what?" he repeated incredulously. "So what?" His

162

lips twisted in an ugly way. "So when were you planning to tell me?"

"You're assuming it's yours?" she retorted, with hard-fought-for coolness. The look that came over Ben's face turned Vichy's blood to ice water.

"Are you looking to get belted?" he snorted. "You know damned well it's mine. Who else could have fathered it?"

"Mark Hartman." The moment his name passed her lips Vichy regretted uttering it. It wasn't fair of her to even verbally involve Mark in this mess. The impact of that name on the man standing in front of her made her doubly sorry she'd mentioned it.

"You *are* looking to get belted," he threatened softly. "Don't push it, Vich. I'm not in the mood to be hassled." He drew a long, calming breath, then said flatly, "We'll get married as soon as possible."

"No!" Vichy exclaimed. "We will not."

"What the hell do you mean, we will not?" Ben rapped sharply.

"Exactly what I say," Vichy retorted, every bit as sharply. "I won't marry you, Ben."

"I'm good enough to go to bed with, but not good enough to marry? Is that it?" Ben nearly shouted, his tone sounding strangely hurt as well as angry.

His response, so traditionally feminine, should have been funny; Vichy wasn't laughing. In fact, she was very close to tears.

"That's it," she concurred over the constriction in her throat. "Now, if that's all you wanted to see me about, I'll be going." She turned, only to have her arm grasped and her body spun back to him.

163

Although it hardly seemed possible, Ben looked more furious than before. "You're not going anywhere," he grated. "At least not until we settle this."

"There's nothing to settle," Vichy cried, attempting unsuccessfully to pull her arm from his grasp. "I'm not going to marry you."

His fingers tightened, yet not enough to cause pain through the heavy material of her coat. "And what about the child?" he demanded.

"It's mine. I'll take care of it." Again Vichy gave a sharp tug of her arm. Again she was unable to free herself. "I want nothing from you."

"You already *have* something from me," Ben corrected her roughly. "And it is as much mine as it is yours, and I want it."

Vichy went numb with a sudden premonition. "What do you mean, you want it?" she asked through lips that had gone bone dry.

"Exactly what I say." Ben's smile closed her throat with fear. His voice matched his smile for grimness. "If you won't share it with me through marriage, I'll take it from you."

"You can't do that!" Vichy cried.

His reply came hard and fast and scathingly. "Do you want to bet?"

"You would say that! No, I don't want to bet, simply because you'd lose."

"No, Vich, I would not." Ben's tone held total conviction.

"But . . . but you can't!" Vichy stared at him in confusion. "How could you? You don't mean you'd try and abduct . . ."

"Don't be ridiculous," he snapped. "I mean I'd sue you for custody. I'd win too," Ben added arrogantly.

He was threatening to take her baby! Her baby! Fighting the panic building in her chest, Vichy managed a scornful snort. "I am, or will be, the baby's mother. No judge is going to award you custody if I countersue. And I will."

"And you'll lose," Ben said confidently. It was his very confidence that shook her. Before she could refute his statement, he began firing questions at her. "Have you any money? Are you employed? Do you have any solid prospects of employment? Can you provide a decent home and environment for the child?"

"I—I . . ." She got no further.

"The answer to every one of those questions is no, and you know it," he cut into her futile attempt at defense. "And every one of those questions would be asked in front of a judge. On the other hand, I can truthfully answer yes to all those questions and more." He smiled almost pityingly, then taunted, "Whom do you think the judge will favor?"

"There's my parents," Vichy cried desperately. "They'll help me."

"Oh, great," Ben scoffed. "You'd lay that kind of responsibility on them at their age." His voice dripped sarcasm. "How very thoughtful of you. You're all heart."

Without her conscious volition, Vichy's free hand moved to cover her still flat abdomen protectively.

"Ben, please, don't do this to me," she begged raggedly. Begging was all she had left. She knew that without any visible means of support, if he carried through with his threat to sue, she would very probably lose.

"How badly do you want this baby?" This time his

tightening fingers caused pain in her arm. Refusing to let him see the pain she was feeling, both mentally and physically, Vichy swallowed the gasp that rose to her lips.

"Very badly," she admitted in a whispery voice. Her tautly held body swayed when he suddenly released her. "Very badly," she repeated hoarsely.

"Badly enough to marry me?" Stepping back, he fixed her with a narrow-eyed stare, closely watching for her reaction. "And sleep with me again?" he asked very softly. His close scrutiny was rewarded when her body jerked spasmodically.

"Ben, I told you—" Vichy began in renewed anger.

"There is no other way in hell you'll get to keep it," Ben cut her off brutally. "Hard as it may be for you to believe, I want this child every bit as badly as you do."

"But why?" she cried despairingly. "You have Chad."

Shrugging dismissively, Ben turned away from her. "You may as well take off your coat and sit down," he advised, lowering his long frame into one of the room's two molded plastic chairs. "It's beginning to look as if you're going to be here awhile."

Although Vichy did remove her coat awkwardly with trembling fingers, she did not sit down. She could not; she was far too tense, too nervous. Standing before him, her hands clasped tightly in front of her, Vichy tried again to change his mind by reminding him of his son.

"Ben, you do have Chad," she said with a minimum of control. "Let me have my child."

"All to yourself?" he asked with deceptive quiet. "I'd have no rights at all? No visitation privileges? No say in the way he, or she, is raised?" Ben's lips twisted. "No financial obligations?"

166

For one wild moment Vichy actually thought the idea of having no financial obligations might sway the argument in her favor, but then his expression told her that for one wild moment she wasn't thinking at all. Still, she had to try one more time. "You *do* have Chad," she reminded him frantically.

At first Vichy thought he would make no response at all. Then, to her dismay, she saw a muscle ripple in his jaw an instant before his face settled more harshly into place.

"Yes, I have Chad," Ben replied in a tone every bit as harsh as his expression. "And I am his father in every sense of the word but one." He paused, as if not quite sure if he wanted to go on. Then, in words clear and distinct, he said, "I am not Chad's natural father."

Vichy stared at him in sheer disbelief and confusion. Then she gave a nervous little laugh. "But that's ludicrous! You told me you got custody at the time of the divorce. If he wasn't yours, why would you have . . ."

"I didn't know." His tight voice sliced across hers. "My wife told me in the hall just outside of the room in which the verdict was rendered." He laughed unpleasantly. "She didn't want to be tied down, she said, so she let me believe Chad was mine, knowing I'd fight for him, fight for everything I was worth. She was absolutely right."

Vichy opened her mouth, but he forestalled her questions as though he'd read her mind.

"I had the blood work done. He is definitely *not* mine." His eyes sharpened on her face. "I *will* have my own child, Vich. One way or another. It is entirely up to you."

Vichy felt trapped. Trapped in a motel with a man who was totally unbending. Restlessly, she paced the width of the room, once, twice, raking her mind for a way out. If

167

she could get some money, she thought irrationally, she could disappear. If only . . . Josh! Josh would loan her some money, she knew it!

"May I have some time?" she asked warily, coming to a stop in front of him.

Ben was way ahead of her. "So you can run away again?" he laughed. "You have got to be kidding. I had enough trouble finding you this time. I don't care to repeat the exercise. I'm not your basic Sherlock Holmes type."

"Oh, I'm well aware of that," Vichy retorted. "You're more the basic gambler type."

"What the hell does that mean?" he snapped, backing her up abruptly as he stood up.

"It—it doesn't matter," Vichy answered vaguely, her mind working on something else. "How *did* you find me?" She put her thoughts into words.

"Elementary, my dear," Ben drawled. "First I went to the address you had given me," he paused to smile nastily. "The super told me you'd moved without leaving a forwarding address. That was two weeks ago." He thrust his hands into the pockets of his jeans in a way that left her in little doubt he was fighting the need to shake her, or worse. His stance was intimidating, and Vichy backed up a step. Her movement brought a parody of a smile to his face. "Last weekend I drove back down to Atlantic City." He went on calmly. Too calmly. "I went to the hotel management. They refused to divulge any information at all about you." His smile turned sardonic. "By the time I thought of talking to Ken, I wasn't even sure anymore why I wanted to find you."

"But Ken didn't have my parents' address!" Vichy exclaimed.

"But Ken did know the name of your agent," Ben shot back.

"Bernie!"

"Yes, Bernie," Ben retorted. "I flew back out to California yesterday. He didn't want to say anything at first but, after I'd convinced him we'd had a lovers' quarrel, he opened up. He told me all about how you had decided to quit the entertainment business and go home to stay. He also told me where home was." He bowed mockingly. "And here I am, at your service."

"You had no right—" Vichy began angrily.

"I *thought* I had every right," Ben again cut her off harshly. "I *thought* the time we'd spent together gave me that right, at least to an explanation of why you took off without a word the way you did."

Vichy stood perfectly still. It was very close, but then, it was always very close: that memory of Ben's laughing, and the woman so eager to kiss him. Shaking her head to dispel the scene, Vichy looked him straight in the eye and lied, "I—I just decided it was time to go home; the affair was over."

"Affair?" Ben's icy tone chilled her. "Affair?" he repeated cuttingly. "Well, sweetheart," he sneered the endearment, "I'm afraid the 'affair' is going to have to continue. That is, if you want to keep this child."

Everything about him told Vichy that argument would be futile, yet she had to try one more time. "Ben, please, don't go through with this. Can't you see how unfair it would be to the child? I mean, to bring a child into a home where there's dissension just would not be fair."

"And you're so sure there will be dissension?" Ben

rapped. "We weren't doing too badly in that motel room, you know."

Not as long as I was foolishly believing that I was your only woman, Vichy cried silently. *How could I bear to live with you, sleep with you, and wonder day and night how many others there are?* Aloud, all she said was, "I don't want to get married. I've *been* that route. I didn't like the scenery."

"Damn it, Vich!" Ben exploded. "I didn't give you a rough time, he did. If we both work at it, we can make a go of it. We have to." He sighed, and for a fleeting second Vichy thought she saw a hint of sadness, or disappointment, flicker over his face. Then it was gone and his expression was harsher. "Besides which," he sighed again, "there's no other way. You want the child. I want the child. We will just have to share it . . . legally."

Still Vichy argued. For over an hour she ranted, raved, and even cried, all to no avail. Ben remained adamant; he would not bend. Either she married him, or she fought him in court. In the end she gave in, as he very likely knew she would.

"All right, all right!" she shouted, when she finally realized he was not going to budge. "I'll marry you, damn you, but don't blame me if we wind up in a divorce court." That she sounded childish, she knew, but at that point she no longer cared. Never had she encountered such an exasperating man!

"How charmingly you accept my proposal," Ben snarled. "If we do wind up in a divorce court, it won't be because I haven't tried." He turned away as if he could no longer bear the sight of her. "We'll get the ball rolling tomorrow morning," he said when he turned back to her.

His face was now washed clean of all expression and his tone was flat, deadly flat. "We'll get married as soon as it is legally possible."

"Tomorrow morning!" Vichy repeated, stunned. "But —but surely you want to go home and prepare Chad, don't you?"

"Chad will accept whatever I tell him," Ben informed her arrogantly. "When I go home, you will be with me. I really hate to say that I don't trust you, Vich, but, I don't." His tone took on iron determination. "I will stay right here, in this very room, until after we are married."

"I am not going to run away, Ben," Vichy sighed. "I know when I'm beaten."

"Sure," he snorted. "Nevertheless, I'll stay here. I think we'll do it Saturday. Now, put your coat on and we'll get things started."

"What can we do tonight?" Vichy squeaked. He was moving much too fast for her and the strain showed in her voice.

"Tell your parents," Ben told her coolly, shrugging into a beautiful vicuna jacket.

"I'll tell them," Vichy said shakily, beginning to panic. "You don't have to go with me."

"I know I don't *have* to go with you," Ben retorted, "but I am going. I helped make it, I'll face your family with you."

Half sick to her stomach, Vichy drove back to her parents' home, Ben, in the Grand Prix, right on her tail. She found both her parents and Bette in the kitchen having a before-bed cup of chocolate. Bette's cheeks flared red when she saw Ben, and her glance shied away from

171

Vichy's. Biting her lip, Vichy fumbled for words to tell them about her condition.

"Mom, Dad, I—I—"

"Vich is pregnant," Ben said flatly over her inept stammering. "We are going to get married."

As subtle as a machine gun, Vichy thought, inwardly wincing at the expressions of shock her parents could not disguise. Surprisingly, they rallied quickly.

"It happens in the best of families," Luke murmured dryly after a short, tense silence. Getting to his feet, he extended his hand to Ben.

"I'm sorry for my bluntness," Ben apologized, accepting Luke's handshake. "But I figured the best way to get it done was to do it."

Strangely, at least Vichy thought it strange, Luke seemed to not only understand, but to agree with Ben.

"Know what you mean," Luke nodded. "So, when are you to going to tie the knot?"

"Saturday," Ben replied.

"It's best." Luke again nodded.

During this exchange Vichy, Johanna, and Bette stared from one to the other in confusion.

"Well, Johanna, don't you have anything to say?" Luke prodded his wife out of her near trance.

"What's to say?" Johanna asked calmly. "It seems to me you and Ben have already said it all." She drew a deep breath, which told Vichy she was not nearly as calm as she pretended to be. "I would have preferred a different, more conventional wedding for Vichy, but, as you say, these things do happen." She blinked and swallowed hard, and Vichy found herself blinking rapidly. "What plans have you made?" she glanced from Vichy to Ben.

172

"None really," Vichy admitted.

"Other than to get married as soon as possible," Ben added. "I have a young son at home and I would like to get back to him by the beginning of next week." His smile held heartwarming charm. "I know he is going to love Vich every bit as much as I do."

Vichy had to gulp back the gasp that rose to her lips. How dare he stand there and lie to her parents like that! When just a few weeks ago he had been celebrating with another woman! Fighting down the urge to slap his lying mouth, Vichy said quickly, "And I know I'm going to love him." *I at least mean what I say,* she thought smugly. *I will try very hard to be a good substitute mother.*

Ben stayed for over an hour. Johanna made more hot chocolate, then, the five of them sitting around the kitchen table, they discussed what Vichy and Ben would have to do before they could get married. Although Ben insisted they wanted no fuss, he finally gave in to Johanna's insistence that a small family party be held after the ceremony.

By the time Vichy got into bed, she was so tired she immediately fell into a deep sleep, only to toss and turn most of the night with dreams of herself decked out in full bridal attire, walking down the aisle while a church full of beautiful women laughed and took turns kissing Ben.

Vichy went to the breakfast table the next morning bleary-eyed and dull-witted. She and her mother were alone in the kitchen, as her father was hiding out in the barn and Bette had long since left to go back to school.

"You'd better have something to eat," Johanna advised, glancing at the clock. "Ben will be here in less then an hour."

How did it happen, Vichy wondered, that her mother

173

spoke so easily of Ben? Oh, he had been utterly charming to her, as well as to her father and Bette, but Vichy had always thought both her parents were shrewd judges of character. Yet all three of them seemed to look on him as something special. Of course, they didn't know him the way she did, she told herself, conveniently forgetting she had thought him very special until the last night of her engagement at the hotel.

"I called Mattie and Josh a little while ago." Johanna startled her with that bit of news. "They will both be here early Saturday morning."

Vichy had to swallow to dislodge the tightness in her throat. "What did they say? Did you tell them that I'm pregnant?"

"Yes, of course I told them," Johanna sighed. "What could they say? I think Josh was more shocked than Mattie." She shook her head. "I really believe Josh thought of you as above that sort of thing."

Vichy winced and averted her suddenly teary eyes. God, she hated to disillusion Josh. He had always been so protective of her. So very much the big brother.

"Now don't go feeling bad about Josh," Johanna admonished, correctly reading Vichy's emotions. "He'll be fine as soon as he takes the time to think. We are all merely human, Vichy. Getting pregnant by the man you love is nothing to be ashamed of." Slipping an arm around her shoulders, she gave her a quick hug, then scolded, "Now eat something. You and Ben have a lot to do."

That week Vichy was to learn that when Ben set his mind to something, he didn't fool around. They drove into Reading to apply for the marriage license and went direct-

174

ly to a lab for the required blood tests after leaving the courthouse.

Tuesday they paid a visit to Vichy's family doctor for their physical examinations. No sooner had she finished introducing Ben to the man who had helped bring her into the world then Ben startled her by a request.

"Could you prescribe something for Vich for morning sickness?" he asked very smoothly.

Having been around for a long time, Dr. Rightmeyer received the news of Vichy's pregnancy with aplomb. "Let's have a look at you," he said to her quietly, ushering her into his examining room.

"How did you know I had morning sickness?" Vichy demanded as they left the office some thirty minutes later, the prescription for pills to control the vomiting in her hand.

"Bette," Ben said unconcernedly. "She told me that's how she'd discovered it."

Although Vichy resented his take-over attitude, she was relieved at the cessation of the racking heaves every morning.

Saturday dawned clear and bitter cold, and Vichy wanted nothing more then to burrow under her covers and escape the day. She loved Ben. If possible more now than before. But she was selfish as far as he was concerned, and the idea of possibly having to share him with others was a torment she would just as soon not have to go through.

The arrival of Mattie and her family drew her out of her bed with a sigh of resignation.

Josh and his family arrived thirty minutes after Mattie and the house rang with voices, all talking at the same time, all, including Josh, teasing Vichy unmercifully. Her family may have been initially shocked at the news of her pregnancy and the need for a hurried wedding, but they were a close unit and they had closed ranks protectively around her.

In midafternoon they made a three-car convoy as they drove to the district justice's office. Ben was waiting for them and Vichy made hurried introductions before they went inside. In less than fifteen minutes it was over, and Vichy's finger was adorned with a plain band of gold that proclaimed her Ben's wife.

The party began as soon as they got back to the house. Vichy, in an effort to avoid close contact with Ben, kept herself busy helping her mother with the food and her father with the drinks—which seemed to flow very freely. At one point she observed Ben in deep conversation with Mattie. At another, she saw Josh and Ben with their heads together. Quite sure her big brother and sister were cautioning Ben on taking care of her, Vichy steered clear of both conferences.

Vichy went cold all over when Ben declared it was time for them to leave. Moving stiffly, she went to her room to get her coat and overnight case—the only case that had not been stashed in the hatchback of her car. Fighting tears, she glanced slowly around the only room she had ever really thought of as hers and then, turning away quickly, she walked out and closed the door.

Their leavetaking was prolonged and noisy, but finally Vichy was behind the wheel of her car following Ben's Grand Prix to the motel.

As she trailed his red taillights, it suddenly hit Vichy that other than somewhere in central New Jersey, she hadn't the vaguest idea of where she was going. The plan

176

had been for them to stop at the motel for Ben's things and then drive straight through to his home, Vichy following him in her own car. So, when they reached the motel, Vichy remained behind the wheel and frowned at Ben when he came around to her door and opened it.

"I'll wait here," she said tersely.

"I've changed my mind," Ben informed her coolly. "It's too late to start home today. We'll stay here tonight and get an early start in the morning."

"B-but—" Vichy stuttered, suddenly very, very nervous.

"I'm too tired to argue, Vich," Ben sighed, swinging the door wide. "Just get out of the car . . . please."

Knowing procrastination would be futile, Vichy slid from behind the wheel, thankful that the room had two beds.

"You may have the bathroom first," Ben offered as soon as the door had closed behind them.

Not about to argue, Vichy opened her valise, removed her nightwear, and dashed into the bathroom. She drew out her shower and nightly routine as long as possible and then, belting her robe securely, she walked back into the bedroom and stopped in her tracks.

CHAPTER TWELVE

Ben, looking tall and lean and altogether too naked in nothing but very brief shorts, was turning from one of the beds where he had just folded back the covers.

"You look tired," he said softly, his eyes making a minute inspection of her face. With a wave of his hand he indicated the bed. "Why don't you turn in?"

The sight of him unnerved her and, breathing carefully, she murmured, "I am not sleeping with you, Ben."

"Why not?" he asked even more softly. "You enjoyed sleeping with me before."

"Yes," Vichy snapped. "Before I realized I was expected to share you with others."

Ben went rigid, a frown drawing a dark line between his brows. "I think you had better explain that remark," he rapped sharply.

His tone flicked her on the raw. How dare he play the

innocent? she riled silently. Standing stiffly erect, she glared at him defiantly. He was totally unimpressed.

"I'm waiting, Vich," he ground out, sounding like a man who was hanging on to his patience by sheer willpower. Moving slowly, he crossed the room to stand in front of her, his eyes warning dire things if she did not speak quickly.

Vichy was suddenly very tired. She had been living on her nerves for weeks. Now, when she needed them most, her nerves gave up the battle. Closing her eyes wearily, she began speaking in a flat monotone.

"I was married when I was twenty-two. A very young, dumb twenty-two."

"What does that have to do—" Ben stopped speaking when Vichy went on as if she hadn't heard him.

"Although there is no resemblance whatever between you and Brad, he loved to gamble, much the same as you do."

"Now, wait a minute!" Ben exclaimed, but again she went on, his protest unheard.

"We were married six months. I was working one of the smaller rooms in Vegas and, again much the same as you, he showed up every night for my final set. Until that last night."

Here she stopped her narrative to open her eyes and stare at him. When she continued, her voice was even lower, flatter. "I hadn't even realized the parallel but, exactly like you, he did not show up that last night. And exactly like that last night in Atlantic City with you, I was not concerned." Vichy paused to smile humorlessly. "The difference was, unlike that last night in Atlantic City, I did not find Brad in the casino. I didn't even look for him

179

there." Her smile disappeared. "Positive he was planning a private celebration of our six-month-old marriage, I rushed to our room."

Vichy had Ben's undivided attention now. As if sensing what was coming, he was hanging on to her every word.

"Wanting to surprise him, I inserted the key and unlocked the door to our room soundlessly. When the door swung open, the bottom fell out of my life. The light was on, and Brad was in bed, but he wasn't asleep, and he wasn't alone." A shudder of remembrance shook her slender body and, with a muttered curse, Ben's hand grasped her upper arms.

"Vichy, stop."

This time his fingers inflicted no pain, for though his hold on her was firm, it was also tenderly protective. His tone reflected the emotions guiding his hands.

Ignoring his command, Vichy went on tonelessly. "The woman was a cocktail waitress in the lounge, and she was beautiful. They were in bed."

"Vichy, stop!"

This time his emotion-roughened voice drew her eyes to his. His were dark red with concern. Hers were opaque with sadness.

"Vichy." Ben's hands moved, giving her a gentle shake. "I'm sorry for what you had to go through, but I do not see what it has to do—" He broke off, his gaze narrowing on her face. "You said, 'Unlike that last night in Atlantic City, you did not find Brad in the casino.' What did you mean?"

"I did find you," she answered wearily.

"I don't understand," Ben shook his head. "I didn't see you again after you told me to get lost."

"I know, but I saw you." Now the blue eyes that gazed at him were misty with tears. "You were standing at the cashier's cage, having just cashed in chips to the tune of thirty-four thousand dollars. You were not alone. There was a young woman with you. She had her arms around your waist, and you were laughing and kissing each other."

"Vichy, for God's sake, that—"

"While I watched you I could see that hotel room, that bed." The low monotone was gone. With every other word Vichy's voice rose, building to an anguished cry.

"Only it wasn't Brad on that bed. Brad doesn't matter anymore. It was you I saw, Ben, you. And the pain I felt was unbearable."

"Vichy!"

"I couldn't stand it, Ben." Vichy was sobbing now, her arms wrapped tightly around her midsection as if to hold herself together. "Oh, God, Ben, I still can't stand it."

"Oh, good Lord." Ben's groan was a plea, not a curse. Sliding his arms around her, he pulled her against him, holding her tightly, as if to contain and absorb the sobs that shook her.

"Vichy, listen to me, listen," Ben said urgently. "That woman was Mike's wife, Shelly. Are you listening?" He felt her head move up and down, then he went on quietly. "She and Mike found me at the craps table just about the time I'd decided to quit while I was ahead. They had been looking for me throughout most of the day. If you hadn't run, if you had come to me, you'd have found Mike standing three feet away, grinning his damn fool head off." He bent his head and she felt his lips move against her hair. "If you had only come to me."

181

"Oh, Ben," Vichy moaned into his chest. "I could not have walked to you then. You can't imagine what I was feeling." Her weeping had subsided into hiccuping sobs.

"I have an idea." His arms tightened crushingly. "I know the rage and pain I felt when you intimated you had been with Mark Hartman." His voice dropped to a raspy growl. "You were lying, weren't you?"

Her murmured response was barely audible, but the affirmitive motion of her head was all the answer he required. Lowering his head farther, his lips brushed over her temple, then over her ear.

"I love you, Vichy," Ben whispered fervently. "I didn't know what to do when I couldn't find you that night. Then, when I went back to our room and found your bracelet and necklace on the bed and realized you'd gone" —his voice held a raw note, and Vichy felt the shudder that rippled through his long body—"I—I thought I'd go crazy. And then, when I couldn't find you in California . . ." His one hand came up to tangle in her disheveled mass of dark hair. Tugging gently, he forced her head back until he could stare into her tear-blurred eyes.

"After what you just said, you don't have to tell me you love me. I know you do. But I want to hear it just the same."

"I love you, Ben, desperately."

Her avowal, her parted, trembling lips proved too much for him. With a groaned "Oh, God, Vichy," he fastened his mouth onto hers.

Scooping her up into his arms, Ben carried her to the bed. "I've been like a wildman these last weeks," he murmured as he lay down beside her. "I haven't slept worth

182

a damn." His lips teased hers into supplication. "I'd grown too used to waking and finding you beside me."

His tongue snaked out, searching for hers. Ben was quiet for some seconds as his lips, his tongue tasted the sweetness of her mouth. "I need you, Vichy. I forget how to live when I'm away from you. Love me, sweetheart. I'm so empty. Fill me with your love."

Ben's hands, moving with urgent restlessness over her responding body, evoked a familiar wildness in Vichy. Gasping his name over and over, she lost herself in the madness that seemed to affect them both in equal measure.

Time, place, the rest of the world lost all meaning as she took him to herself as greedily as he possessed her. With her mouth and her body and her enfolding arms and legs, she immersed herself in the sensuousness of Ben's driving need of her.

It was very late when Vichy stirred inside the warm circle of Ben's arms.

"Are you cold?" he whispered.

"No," Vichy moved her face against his hair-rough chest. "I'm—I'm frightened."

"Frightened?" Ben echoed in astonishment. His body stiffened, then jerked as he flipped her onto her back where he could look into her face. "Frightened of what?" His tone reflected the baffled expression on his face.

"I was married to a gambler before, Ben," Vichy sighed. "I can't stand the idea of living my life on the highs and lows of the careless toss of a pair of dice."

"What the hell is this?" Jackknifing into a sitting position, Ben turned and grasped her naked shoulders to hold her flat and still. "I am not a gambler. I enjoy gambling

183

occasionally, simply for the challenge. Lord, Vichy, life itself is a gamble."

"Are you telling me you don't gamble compulsively?" Vichy asked warily.

"Hell, no!" Ben exploded. "I told you I have a job. If you had asked, I'd have told you how I earn my living."

"But I thought it was just any old job, meaningless and unimportant," Vichy cried. "A stop-gap for when the dice or cards are cold for you."

"Good grief, I don't believe this!" Ben exclaimed, shaking his head. "Vichy, I'm a research scientist."

"A what!" Vichy's eyes flew wide in astonishment.

"A scientist," Ben nearly shouted. "Does the name Princeton ring a bell?"

"Princeton?" Vichy repeated dumbly. Then, her eyes widening even more, she whispered, "*The* Princeton?"

"The very same," Ben drawled dryly.

"And that's where we're going tomorrow?" she asked hesitantly.

"You got it." Ben's tone now held amusement.

Vichy bit her lip in consternation, feeling unbelievably stupid. "Then that's why you were free to be in Atlantic City that first week?" she had to ask, even though she already knew the answer.

"Right on center," Ben nodded, obviously fighting laughter. "I was on Thanksgiving break."

"Oh, Ben," Vichy wailed. "To think I almost threw it all away! I feel like such a fool."

Her tone washed all sign of amusement from his face. Releasing his hold on her shoulders, Ben slid his hands out along the bed until he was spread-eagle on top of her.

Touching her lips gently with his, he kissed her lingeringly.

"I love you," he whispered when he lifted his head.
"And I don't care if you are a fool." His smile took her
breath away. "As long as you are *my* fool."

The house, just off campus, was quiet and dark, except
for a dim light in the small, centrally located room on the
second floor. The leaves on the tree outside the room's one
window, their brilliant fall colors reduced to a solid mass
of black, rustled dryly in the pre-dawn breeze.

Inside the room the silence was broken by the rhythmic
creak of rocking chair runners on the carpeted floor, and
a muted, gurgling sound.

Sitting in the rocking chair, a softly tender smile on her
face, Vichy gazed down lovingly at her hungrily feeding,
perfectly beautiful infant daughter.

In her gulping greed, the source of the milky flow was
lost, and her tiny bud lips opened in a wail of frustration.
Her smile deepening, Vichy raised a hand to her breast to
reinsert the nipple inside her daughter's searching mouth.

"Slow down, you little pig," she murmured laughingly.
"As your pop-pop would tell you: The faster you go, the
behinder you get."

A soft chuckle drew her bemused glance to the door-
way. Leaning lazily against the door frame, wearing only
a pair of tight faded blue jeans that looked like they'd been
spray-painted onto the lower half of his body, Ben
watched the feeding ritual.

As her eyes touched him, Vichy was struck by the
expression on his face. She had seen an expression almost
exactly like that before, but where?

"I'm sorry, darling, did we wake you?" Vichy asked softly.

"No." Ben's tone matched hers for softness. "I woke up and got to missing you." His eyes remained fastened on his daughter's ecstatic face. "I'm jealous of her, you know." Ben made the admission without inflection.

"Jealous!" Vichy gasped. "Don't be silly, Ben."

"I mean it," he insisted calmly. "Every time she stakes a claim on a part of you that I consider within my own territorial rights, I feel a stab of jealousy."

Vichy felt her cheeks grow warm with a combination of embarrassment and pleasure. She didn't know why she still blushed so readily at his outrageousness. She certainly knew by now that Ben said whatever was on his mind. If her husband was nothing else, he was open and completely honest. Of course, she had learned over the last months that he was much more than that. The words tender, gentle, loving, and considerate jumped into her mind.

"Well, you have one consolation, love," she said soothingly, teasingly. "Her claim is only temporary. You hold lifetime rights."

At her soft assurance he lifted his eyes to hers and the breath caught in her throat. The expression on his face was the same as before, only now Vichy knew where she'd seen it before, and what it meant.

She had caught that same kind of expression on Mattie's husband's face several times when he had thought he was unobserved. The expression was one of near adoration.

Trembling with reaction of her discovery, Vichy studied Ben's visage more thoroughly. More fully defined, his expression proclaimed more than love. Embodied within

186

that expression was total commitment of heart, mind, and soul.

Shaken to the depths of her being, Vichy blinked against the onrush of warm moisture to her eyes. Ben could not miss seeing the gathering tears.

"Are you happy, sweetheart?" he asked anxiously, crossing the floor to stand before her.

"I'm very much afraid," Vichy whispered huskily, "that if I get any happier, I'm going to explode into a million pieces of joyousness."

Ben's relieved laughter surrounded her like a close embrace. Bending over the rocking chair, he kissed her tenderly on the lips, whispering, "I couldn't have put my own feelings into better words."

LOOK FOR NEXT MONTH'S
CANDLELIGHT ECSTASY ROMANCES™